The Stately Pantheon

Kirsty Neary

A Wild Wolf Publication

Published by Wild Wolf Publishing in 2009

Copyright © 2009 Kirsty Neary

First print

ISBN: 978-0-9562114-3-9

www.wildwolfpublishing.com

"Here was a panacea, a nepenthe, *for all human woes; here was the secret of happiness, about which philosophers had disputed for so many ages, at once discovered; happiness might now be bought for a penny, and carried in the waistcoat pocket; portable ecstasies might be had corked up in a pint bottle; and peace of mind could be sent down in gallons by the mail-coach. But, if I talk in this way, the reader will think I am laughing; and I can assure him, that nobody will laugh long."*

Thomas de Quincy, *Confessions of an English Opium Eater*

Dear Martin ... enjoy the book, & remember... it's not an instruction manual, hehe!

lots of love,

Kirsty

Part I

They meet at the subway station under the bridge, between the cigarette stand and the turnstile. Covert operations like these require a swift get-away.

Lance wears a pinstripe suit from Savile Row beneath his overcoat. This is lined not only with the finest silk, but with capacious secret pockets for the movement of contraband. Hilary, swept tightly into chignon and Prada, is out for blood and losing patience. A pit-stop at the ATM reveals an unaccountable deficit. The woman on the machine's diminutive video screen spreads into a shit-eating digital grin, mocking Hilary's lack of funds, her mounting serotonin re-uptake.

Lance looks over her padded shoulders, frowning.

"Are we in a spot of trouble?"

"I've got enough for the stuff, tonight. But nothing for the rest of the week. I can't ask my guy for any more on tick."

Lance looks up, any hopeful skyward glances panned back by the murky underside of the bridge.

Deep shadow can't obscure the graffiti, scratched and sprayed high enough to provoke curiosity as to how it got there, unnoticed. Like everything else in the city, it went on under cover of darkness, into the vanishing points of blind eyes.

"Just take what you can, I'll figure something else out. Hurry up, the show's starting soon, and I want a drink before we get in."

Hilary reluctantly clicks to max out her account, and grabs the wad of cash in a vengeful claw, acrylics biting flesh. Folding half of it into her pocket-book, she inhales deeply, consigning the scent of money to her memory bank for the last time in what will now be a while. She passes the other half to Lance.

"Here's your share. Give me a taste."

Lance places the money into an inside pocket on the left side of the coat, and from the right withdraws a small matchbox, wrapped in a page from an FHM magazine.

Hilary holds in to her ear and rattles gently, the space inside whispering back like a seashell. There's enough in there for tonight, at least until intermission. It slips down the slick of her nylons, into the side of her leather boot.

They're ready. Perhaps not furnished as they'd have preferred, but ready.

Emerging from the subway, they blink away neon aftermath and make their way to the venue. Stepping over excrement, polystyrene takeaway boxes, streams of piss and the odd inert vagrant, Lance grumbles. He's rarely out on foot in the city, and it's gotten no better since teenage sprees of fifteen years ago. He attempts to flag down a taxi, despite the theatre's looming presence visible on the next block. The cab-drivers ignore him, hustling along the queue from the stance leading from the other end of the street. Lance grabs Hilary's arm, hurrying her along. The tick of her high heels along the pavement ascends to a frantic shriek, ceasing only when they reach the scratched marble staircase ascending to the Pantheon Theatre.

It's fortunate that Lance has been here before. They'd have walked past it otherwise – nestled between a pub and an abandoned pawnshop, it's a sliver of a place, an absolute mockery of its namesake in terms of girth. The double doors leading onto the lobby occupy most of the breadth. The height of the terraced building stretches up at least four floors, but Hilary can't imagine where they're keeping the auditorium – it's a ridiculously skinny cuboid, at least five times taller than it is wide. Three rows of old-fashioned sliding windows loom over the upper floors, interspersed with smaller portholes of cloudy glass, giving the overall impression of a trio of skinny, grinning Cyclops peeking from a club sandwich.

It's an evening of dual gratification – Polly's play will no doubt be awful, but the contacts to be made there are priceless, not to be passed up in a hurry. They'd decided to skip the pre-theatre meal, settling for something more reliable, more satisfying. All that jittering through that hour before a hit is bad enough, without the chink of plates and cutlery, the hyper-bright Rorschach blots of puree and jus spattering napkins and chins.

The lobby flashes past quickly, as the tickets exchange hands. Once in the body of the theatre, they grab a spot at the bar.

Before dashing for the bathrooms, they take a look around. It's an amalgam of claustrophobia and ample space. The recesses in the vaulted ceilings are spacious, but the darkness therein implies closed quarters, unattainable heights. The teak bar-top and stools, the booths lining the room, keep the clientele pinned in a regimented series of cells and screened compartments. Groups of theatre-goers add to the effect, huddling in small groups, brandishing martini glasses close to the waist, like shotguns.

Paranoia creeps, and must be addressed as quickly as humanly possible. Quasi-human faces leer from the frescoes bedecking the walls, compounding the sensation of being watched. Lance gestures to the passage leading to the restrooms, the trembling in his hands offset by the forgiving mood lighting from over the gantry.

"You'd better go first. You always take ages anyway."

The bathroom door is heavy dark wood, panelled with wrought-iron inserts, imprisoning the golden cookie-cutter female screwed between. It gives onto a row of stalls, with full-length doors. Cisterns remain evident, a rare convenience when these days, every bathroom seems keen to hide them behind walls, operated by a motion-sensor. One by one, the public houses and malls strive to remove this offending evidence that the clientele might, actually, take a shit.

Hilary taps out a line, rolls up a strip of the magazine and inserts the end of the resulting tube into her left nostril. Taking care to avoid scratches from her false nails, she presses closed her right, and inhales the powder with a delicate sniff. She licks a finger and rubs it along the porcelain, then tamps the resultant fragments onto her lower gum. Turning, she perches on the toilet seat and takes a compact mirror from her handbag, checking for residue. With a vermilion wax pencil, she traces an outline just outside the natural boundary of her lips, filling them in with a lipstick of the same shade.

Flushing the toilet, and with it the scrunched magazine wrapper, she emerges from the cubicle to take a look at the overall effect in the full-length mirror.

Fucking magic. She tilts her head appreciatively, the dunt having removed any cause to notice the slight darkening of her lower lids, the quarter-inch of brunette edging from her hairline into the honey-blonde. She's not bad for thirty-five. Everything in its right place, gravity notwithstanding. She blows an air-kiss at her reflection, smoothes her pencil skirt over her toned thighs, and struts back into the bar.

Lance is grinning, his face half-way down a pint glass. He has evidently taken advantage of the slow crowding of the bar and his resulting inconspicuousness to run ahead with it. A glass of white wine glimmers above the barstool over which her blazer jacket is slung, and she sits down to writhe a little in the waking of sensation. As the initial edge wears off, Hilary has to know whether the evening has the promise she hopes for.

"So? Are we alright for later?"

"I spoke to one of her minions at the stage door. The great playwright has deigned to meet us after the show…an arrangement can be made."

"Thank Christ. That's some good stuff. You sure that's all you have on you?"

"Tut, tut, Hilary – you should know that a gentleman does not discuss his assets when in company. And a lady like yourself should know better than to ask."

"Bastard."

"All you need to know is that there's more where that came from. Drink up, dear."

There's ten minutes to go before the performance begins. Lance and Hilary say nothing to each other, they don't have to. Buoyed up on the wheeling, the swift and unchecked magnificence of themselves and everything around, nothing can be permitted that will detract from the high that accompanies this utter immersion.

A soft bell chimes out from the theatre door. It's show-time.

It's predictably dreadful. It doesn't help that neither of the pair can sit still, nor that drinks are forbidden from the performance space. There's no discernable storyline. A trio of mimes, faces painted scarlet instead of the usual white, mimic the dismantling of a bomb to the sound of an apocalyptically sonorous double-bass. An obese woman in a tribal-print bikini sings an aria over some ill-conceived jungle music, her girth adding to the overall impression of a painful and drawn-out labour. Two young women with acid-pink Mohawks, dressed in twin-sets and pearls, weep loudly as they strip to their underwear over the clang and shred of a car-crash. By the time the curtain falls over the ugliness, Hilary has managed to chew a furrow in her lower lip, despoiling her earlier efforts in the bathroom.

As the lights go up, the pair rise from their seats and funnel through the aisle to the bar. They hang back at the doorway, awaiting the emergence of Polly and her entourage, hoping for as brief an autopsy as possible in the aftermath of the play.

Polly is present in clamour before corporeality, wafting a shriek of laughter and cloud of sandalwood perfume through the open stage door. Her slight stature and wispy-eyed myopia do not detract from the unassailable entrance of a powerful woman. Her five feet in height, and, it seems, girth, bedecked from head to toe in bolts of jewelled silk in colours rivalled only by the gaudy streaks running through her hair, commands attention. A huge enamelled brooch in the shape of a ladybird nestles in the hollow her throat, as if taking charge of the orations flying thick and fast. She throws no theatrical hand gestures, being otherwise occupied with the terrified white rabbit clutched between her talons. The creature's wide eyes scream silently, deploying its only remaining weapon: dropping neat little nuggets of shit, unnoticed, down her sari and into the depressions of her pointed harem shoes.

Hilary hisses into Lance's ear.

"*This* is the woman who's supposed to sort us out? Are you out of your mind?"

"Dear, I'm perfectly aware you're used to sourcing from your well-heeled boarding school alumni. However, we find ourselves in desperate times, and these call, it would appear, for a different approach."

"Christ, Lance, this isn't what I had in mind! That play was bad enough, but fucking hell...*look* at her!"

"We wouldn't want to call judgements on first impressions, now, would we? I've heard she's remarkably astute, for such an...interesting lady."

The whispered conversation ceases as the subject sweeps her way toward the speakers, adorers parting like foam before an ocean liner.

"Why, if it isn't Lance Carntyne! And you must be Hilary," she says, squeezing plumed words from between fuchsia lips. "Darling Lance speaks of you *so* often; I feel we must be dear friends already."

Hilary surreptitiously grinds a spiked heel into the meat of Lance's foot, and extends a slim hand to the heap of jangling excess standing a little too far into her personal space. Polly will have none of it, though, and with one arm locked around the petrified rabbit, throws the other around Hilary, smearing her cheek with pink grease.

"We don't shake hands here, dear, we never know what we will catch, tee-hee!"

"Erm...Polly, we're here about a matter of...some importance," says Lance, recovering his bearings.

"Of course, of course. We shall grab a drink from that lovely barman, and you shall join me in my lounge upstairs."

Polly waddles over to the bar, steps on the lower rung of the stool, and dislodges a nearly-full bottle of bourbon from the gantry. Slipping the optic off the neck, she hands it to the barman and says,

"Just take it from the ticket sales, won't you, sweetheart?"

Mike stares, wide-eyed, before nodding like a marionette. He wishes he'd skipped the grass and gone for something stronger. Polly places the rabbit on the counter.

"Boris can stay down here for a while. Just keep him away from the Scotch; we don't want a repeat performance of last time!"

She sweeps away in a tinkle, leaving the staff gaping in her wake.

Hilary and Lance follow Polly through the crowd, and smile haughtily at the last faces before Polly swings the stage door closed. They follow her up several rickety flights of stairs, and eventually stand before another heavy door, padlocked and mortised. Polly withdraws a loop of keys, and begins sliding bolts and clicking locks.

"Welcome to my humble abode," she chirps, and throws open the door to a luscious bordello. Dali prints paper the low walls, arching up to an alcove from which falls a chandelier of sparkling glass, the rosy fragments shooting prisms of light across the rest of the room. A hat-stand, laden with feather boas and fur coats and topped with a bowler hat, is lent the appearance of a skinny pimp. Around a cut-glass coffee table, three plump sofas cluster, bedecked in throws of satin and Egyptian cotton. Bookcases stacked with leather-bound volumes brace the outer walls, whilst a huge television screen and entertainment system crouch in what was once a fireplace. Hilary half-expects the appearance of a white tiger from behind one of the settees, but thankfully the menagerie ends with a silver bird-cage in one corner, inside which perch a pair of lollipop-coloured lovebirds. Polly places the bottle on the table.

"Take a seat, dears. Let's get down to business."

10

Carrie waits for the twilight, reluctant to leave under the slack cover of fogged daylight looming outside. Cloud cover is entire, yet, from behind, the sunrays bounce light from the glass roofs of the cityscape to the firmament and back again, again, again. Everything cloys in the damp air and solid light, like utter submersion in a jar of mayonnaise, or a White Russian without the pleasing numbness.

Tonight, it's yet another of Polly's bizarre showcases, some comment or other on mass media and terrorism. Or so says the in-house blurb. Carrie doesn't go for the shows, anymore, but for the safe house away from this shit-hole. Time and patience have not slackened her dislike for Kevin in the slightest. He's certainly endured the longest of her mother's apparently endless string of younger men, but he's still a smarmy arsehole with too much cash and not a smidgen of class. His earlier attempts to charm had fallen flat, about as convincing as his sun-bed tan. Carrie has seen it before, too often, and would much rather avoid him whenever possible - if only to escape the sickening cloy of his knockoff aftershave. Her faux-politeness is driving her mad, and each time she catches her own reflection grinning sycophantically from the frames of his designer sunglasses, only extreme self-control prevents her from knocking them off his pinched-weasel mug.

She seethes quietly at the sound of the front door swinging open. It's not a good sign: he clearly feels he's progressed beyond having to ring the doorbell. She swings her feet off the bed, grabs her canvas knapsack, and empties the contents over the duvet to assess the requirements for an evening's sustenance. A set of keys, a roll of breath mints, a plastic coin purse with enough copper and silver, perhaps, for a fresh packet of cigarettes. A bus pass, expired, but still adequate currency to appease the swift glances of the drivers. A tiny silver snuff box: borrowed without permission from her mother, which contains the makings of two joints, perhaps three if she can make it stretch. A notebook, bound in maroon velvet from the cut-offs of her grandmother's curtains. Most important of all, her identification card: the open door to the theatre, now and forever. She had held onto her father's surname after his disappearance, not through any affection for the great magician, but for the link it kept alive with her grandmother.

Grandma Sherwood had been quite the thespian in her day, filling the rafters of the then-innocuous music hall with her lilting contralto and her flawless Shakespearean orations. When Granddad Sherwood had passed, only forty, in a vaguely-accounted accident at the docks, he had left his wife enough of a legacy to buy the theatre. She re-named it The Pantheon, presumably invoking the grandeur of the Roman archetype. She had transformed it from a dusty house of ill-repute into a beautiful hall of mystery and magic, playing hostess to some of the grandest personalities treading the boards in Glasgow in that honeyed heyday.

After her grandmother's death, Carrie had been too young to understand the ramifications of the legal somersaults passing ownership of the theatre back and forth between contentious parties. In the end, though, a compromise was reached: the property would belong to executors, but the aesthetics would remain with the family. Unfortunately, in the absence of another present and surviving descendent, and Carrie's mother's dearth of interest, there wasn't a platform for any of the Sherwood family to have their say. The executors' decision follows thus: When Carrie turns eighteen in the forthcoming year, there can be changes made, but until then, the reins of the theatre will lie in the capable grasp of Polly Monday, Zinnia Sherwood's oldest and dearest friend.

Carrie isn't yet sure how much of a force she can muster in terms of driving the ship, but in the interim, free access to the building anytime, and a blind eye turned to her samplings from the bar and restaurant, make for rather a plush inheritance.

Tapping out the contents of the snuff box onto the front page of a music magazine, she begins to skin up a joint for consumption on the short walk to the bus stop. She favours cinnamon cigarette papers; the sweet warmth mingling with the sharper tang of the herb, creating an unrivalled taste experience verging on the epicurean.

She needs a dunt, now, too – rolling up the stairwell like a slurry of rotting, swelling compost comes Kevin's gut-churning guffaw. This is the sound of a man three cans down, and unlikely to move for the rest of the evening. She scrapes everything back into her bag, and stands before the bedroom mirror for a half-hearted micro-groom.

She's a pretty girl; at least her mother says she would be if she smiled more often. Nice teeth, courtesy of some tantrum-inducing orthodontics. Pale brown eyes the colour of marmalade; between scaffolds of thick lashes that require no assistance from makeup or prosthetics. She casts these orbs briefly to the window; night is falling, and it's as good a time as any to get going.

Yanking a comb through her thick, dark hair, she tilts her chin forward to examine the development of what promises to be a pimple with some commendable stamina. Thrusting her tongue into her lower lip, she scowls at her reflected image and turns away. Nothing to be done, no point pitching a fit; she'd just expected to have grown out of such sebaceous mutiny by now.

She smiles as she tightens the laces on her Doctor Martens, still undecided as to whether she wears them for their comfort, or because she knows her mother can't stand them. Throwing a camouflage jacket of her father's over her jeans and vintage Cure T-shirt, she's ready. She grabs the shoulder bag, sticks the joint behind her ear and thunders down the stairs. Narrowly avoiding the sleeping feline curled up on the bottom step, she's out the front door before she has to exchange words with either half of the happy couple, who are no doubt immovably snuggled on the sofa for their evening's dose of turgid light entertainment and cheap lager.

Stalking down the sun-starved streets of Carver Village, she pats her pocket for a lighter. Pausing to fire up the spliff, she takes a deep breath, turns away from the leering row of houses and closes her eyes. Grinding gears from passing traffic betrays the proximity of the motorway, lessening the impact of the faux-rural sensibility by the recent ten-foot thick plantation of trees and bushes which flank the drive. Still, if she keeps her line of sight above waist-level, the overall effect is quite pleasant, if only for its contrast to the concrete and dandelion wasteland that constitute the front gardens.

She clambers the low fence, and, leaning against a pliable sapling, soon begins to blow whorls of velvety smoke up into the descending dark.

As the furrows of cloud push impatiently at the earth's circumference, forcing on the impending pitch, the bank of green becomes a field of curiosities. The dome of a monkey-puzzle tree becomes the silhouette of the top half of a grinning skull, with mottled globs of watery twilight for eye sockets. Carrie rolls her shoulder around, steeling herself against the impending weight of the traffic noise at full volume. She extinguishes her canapé against the trunk of the tree, then crosses the street. Rounding the corner onto the main road, she makes it just in time to stick an arm out for an approaching bus, its front lamps turned up too bright to see the route number. It doesn't matter; all roads lead to the city, the only respite from the black holes of the satellite towns. The only forthcoming variation upon disembarking will be which shop she'll enter, to count out her change in exchange for a deck of Camels, and which jaded, exhausted shop clerk will demand, for the millionth time, to see her identification. Thereafter, she can slip from the newsagents or the off-licence, ready for battle, melding back into the anonymity of the night.

Evan is having a great deal of trouble fastening his cravat. He has seen his old man accomplish this as routine for so many years, yet, when called upon to fix his own, the mirror-imaging turns his fingers to ends of flaccid hosepipe.

He has to get a move on; he can't fuck this up. That Polly woman seems nice enough, despite clearly being madder than a sack of lemurs, but he knows better than to turn up late and unkempt to a first shift in a new job.

He's extremely nervous, and hopes the beads of sweat tickling his hairline won't give him away. His mother calls from downstairs, and he jolts, further knotting the stupid thing beyond sense and reason. Tugging at a free end, he tears it off and stuffs it into his chest pocket, thrusting a pissy mouthful of air from between his top lip and teeth.

"Evan! Are you ready yet? I can give you a lift if you hurry up."

"Give me a sec, I'll be right down."

He runs a comb through his wavy copper hair, still a little too long to escape his father's criticism. Flicking the tabs of his shirt collar forward with his thumbs, he grabs his wallet and slinks down the staircase, gliding his rear across the polished banister before thumping to the floor on both feet. His mother waits in the hall, illuminated by the outside lights flicking sparks through the frosted glass of the front door.

"You look very smart, son. Your father would be proud."

"Yeah…I guess. Can you help me with this?" He drags the cravat from his pocket and holds it before his face, sheepishly averting his eyes. "I can't figure it out."

Ms Holmes sighs delicately, luxuriating in that spot of grace which occurs on the rare occasion her grown son asks for her assistance. She takes the strip of dark velvet and moves up close, running her palm along his jaw-line to check for stubble. Butterfly fingers tweak the cravat into a stately loop, in a series of rapid hand movements Evan is at a loss to follow, or repeat.

"There we are. Perfect." She leans forward and grazes his cheek with a peck.

"Aw, mum…!"

She tuts, winks.

"You're never too old for a kiss from your mother."

"Right, right...thanks." God, sometimes he hates himself for allowing such coddling. Then hates himself even more for allowing headspace for such churlish ingratitude.

"Get in the car. It's going to rain, and I don't want you getting those shoes muddy."

Evan trips out to the car, careful to lift his feet carefully to avoid scuffing one shoe on another, giving him a bow-legged goose-step which has his mother, watching from the front door, in silent paroxysms of laughter.

As his mother pulls the car from the drive, Evan feels as though he's leaving behind something more than the house for the evening. This isn't his introduction to the world of work, but it's his first position in the city. Growing up in leafy West Brunswick hadn't exactly presented Vegas-style job opportunities. Sweeping the floor in the local hairdressers and stacking shelves in the village grocery store now seems like such child's play, baby stuff. Here was a job with class; he even had a title instead of an amorphous mixture of all the odd jobs that none of the more senior staff felt were part of their remit. So; being an usher wasn't exactly up there with being a spy, an international playboy or a fighter pilot, but at least it was progress. He'd be in among the theatre classes, the kinds of people his parents feel it's an advantage to get to know. He might even meet famous folk, or at the very least, the odd footballer. The highway streaks past in a flash of blended lights and lurid signs, unnoticed as he drifts into and out of the elegant soirees, the premiers and photo opportunities of whirling fantasy.

As the car glides up to the theatre door, Evan is preparing himself for the red carpet. Smiling wide, he squares his shoulders, takes a deep breath and throws the car door open with such drama that only sheer chance prevents a nasty collision with a passing punter. *Calm down, keep cool,* he admonishes, *don't be such a fucking amateur.*

"Thanks, mum. I'll see you later."

Ms Holmes' lips crinkle in concern. "I don't know how I feel about you being out this late in the city. I keep hearing the most appalling stories."

"Jeez, mum, I'm nearly twenty. I'll be fine."

"Here," she presents him with a ten-pound note. "In case you miss the bus. Don't walk it - get a taxi."

Evan grins at this unexpected bonus, and casts a vague estimate at how many pints it could buy him.

"Cheers, mum. I'll give you it back tomorrow." "Don't worry about it; it's a small price to pay for getting you back safe. When do you think you'll be home?"

"I'll be back late. Don't wait up; just leave the door on the latch."

"Okay...well, good luck, sweetheart."

"Cheerio."

Evan slides from the front seat and saunters to the theatre door, breathing deeply before crossing the threshold into the glassy foyer. The punters are gathered in a solid throng already, throwing pashminas over shoulders, tapping the floor with the spikes of golf umbrellas, smoking menthol cigarettes and chattering in a language he can't understand. Vehemently polysyllabic, multi-hyphenated words drip from glossed mouths, spilling cognac-laced breath into the dizzy air...

"Post-feminism is over, it's all about phallocentrism in the male gaze – she's using dubstep, look at the bluefaces..."

"She's investing much in this Jodorowsky movement..."

"Crowdsourcing is producing a great deal of ficto-reality productions...."

"One could argue the impossibility of gendering the gaze, what with so many emerging genders..."

"Yes, it took a while to arrive, the waiting lists are horrendous...but one can't reasonably argue when it's the scallop-edged quilted Chanel..."

So many clamouring voices, louder and louder, all screaming to be heard, remembered, qualified. Evan quickly arrests the urge to stick his hands into his pockets and lower his head – this is not the place for the merest hint of the slovenly. He makes his way to the archway leading to the staff room, the site of his interview, and raps on the door. An obscenely fat, busty steward stands in the entryway, dressed in a uniform at least thrice the size of Evan's.

"Help ye, mate?" he booms, his entire front aspect wobbling with the thrum of his baritone.

"Erm...my name's Evan Holmes. I'm here for my shift." "Usher, are ye? Grand. Here," he hands Evan a tiny flashlight, and a laminated seating plan. "Name's Joe, main hall's that way, dead easy. Just show the plebs to their seats. Don't let anyone take a drink in; the boss hasn't squared a licence yet. Give me a shout if there are any rabble-rousers. When the hall's empty, sweep the place. There's a cupboard full of cleaning stuff at the back. Any questions?"

Evan shakes his head, tucks the seating plan into his waistcoat pocket, and slips the loop of the flashlight around his wrist. "No...I think I can manage that."

"Right. Enjoy the show, harhar."

Joe places a cigarette between his burst-couch of a mouth, and plops into a swing chair in front of a small television screen. Evan remains in the doorway, in case of further instructions.

Joe glares.

"What you waiting for? Show's on in five minutes."

He extends a foot to the edge of the door, and nudges it. It swings slowly closed in Evan's face. Right. Time to get going.

To his mild displeasure, there turns out to much less work involved than even Joe had specified – instead of respecting the clout of his seating plan and torch, most of the folk sweep right past him and to their seats without assistance. This crowd are, in the main, clearly comprised of regular attendees, going by the assured and arrogant manner with which they stalk the aisles and rows. There are a few awkward-looking types who appear unsure as to what exactly they're doing in a theatre, as though having gotten lost en route to the bookies, but they seem happy enough to be guided by Evan and his flashlight. Thereafter the labour involved comes down to perching on a barstool at the back of the auditorium, watching the show and keeping an eye on the audience's knobbly silhouette for any insurgency. The only minor risk seems to come from the well-dressed couple sitting in the back row aisle seats – they mutter and rustle throughout the first five minutes, to the annoyance of the surrounding spectators. Evan gulps, preparing to ask them to quieten down, but his movements are pre-empted by the hook-nosed, hawk-eyed pair of older women in the row in front.

"Shhhhttt! If yer no gonnae watch the show in peace, the door's back there."

"I do apologise, I didn't know we were being so loud. We'll be quiet," says the gentleman, lowering his head.

Evan awkwardly resumes his seat, and watches the show.

The performance is insane – wild colours, migraine-inducing mix-ups of uncomplimentary genres, and the only naked flesh on show is less than appealing to the discerning punter. A brief flicker of interest sparks in his gut at the sight of a pair of female punks performing a strip, but their shredding wails of despair remove any possible enjoyment of the spectacle. When the lights come up, and he's back on duty, he feels the same out-of-body unreality that sometimes occurs when he jolts awake, after having fallen asleep in the middle of a study session. He holds back from shaking his head in the manner of a wet dog, settling for a wide cracking open of his eyes. Murmuring farewells to the departing audience, he stands at the door, hands clasped behind his back, and awaits for the room to empty for cleaning.

Aside from the odd handful of crumpled papers from smuggled peanut and chocolate wrappers, this proves to be a swift job. Evan sets to it efficiently, jerking trash into the dustpan with the dapper rhythm of a waltz. He's not particularly impressed, having neither seen nor heard any other employee save the less than enthusiastic Joe, but a job's a job. Placing the dustpan back in the cupboard at the rear of the theatre, he opens the stage door and stands, surveying the chattering crowd.

There's Polly, swinging through the throng. She pauses before Evan and asks,

"Everybody out? Everything ship-shape?"

"Erm, yes, I think so…I mean, is there anything else you'd like me to do?"

"No, no, Mr…Holmes, is it? I'm sure you've done a sterling job. More importantly, what did you think of the show?" Her brows narrow, creeping over the top rims of her spectacles. The answer here is clearly a deal-breaker.

"It was…extremely thought-provoking, Ms Monday."

"Call me Polly. And, you like having your…*thoughts provoked*?"

"Yes, yes I do. I'm studying to be a journalist, and I'm keen to learn about the world of theatre and arts, as well as current affairs." He flinches, realising that he's parroting his CV practically to the letter.

Polly moulds her mouth into a saccharine protrusion, an approximation of a contemplative smile.

"In that case, you shall fit into our little family *marvellously*. I realise you've been thrown into the deep end somewhat, this evening, but you've proved you can manage. What do you think? Are you content to join the team?"

"Of course. Thank you!"

She speaks so quickly, so persuasively, rattling off each clause as if pasting it upon him. He doesn't have much choice, even if he hadn't wanted to keep a city job. He's now fairly chuffed; the trickles of nervous sweat had calmed after he'd gotten settled, but that hadn't entirely dispensed with the fear that this entire thing was a fluke. Now he had a definite position. Now he's a part of the city night.

"We'll draw up contracts and so forth another time, I'm dreadful with paperwork, and I have an appointment with some customers this evening. Same time, same place tomorrow, does that suit?"

"It does indeed, Ms...I mean, Polly."

"There's a drink waiting for you at the bar – all staff are entitled to a complimentary beverage with each shift. You may have it anytime, but most prefer to take it at the end, instead of before or during. Just tell that lovely barman what you're after and he'll sort you out."

"Sure, thank you. That's very kind."

"Dear, that's the way we do things here. Happy staff makes for a far superior theatrical experience, and that's my undiluted agenda in this house of mirth."

With that, she turns to the couple from earlier on, who wait at the table nearest the stage door. He is dismissed. He heads for the bar – his head is still spinning vaguely, and he could use that drink.

There's a girl at the bar tying knots in a plastic straw, one arm on the counter, one resting on a thick black book. This occupies her for the first few sips of Evan's pint, until she runs out of space in the length of plastic. She drops it to the marble counter, and moves on to inserting an impressive number of cocktail sticks into a maraschino cherry. What gets him is the rapture, the sheer malevolent concentration with which she imbues the enterprise. That paltry globe of synthetic scarlet seems to be taking the heat for some wider, as yet unexplored grievance. She either has trouble, or more likely, *is* trouble. She drops her tiny talisman into an empty martini glass, narrowing her eyes as she senses the gaze of another pair. She jerks her head, turning to catch him square in the eye, without any preliminary searching in the crowd. She has a hunter's instinct, perhaps hunted.

"What are you looking at, pal?"

She speaks without inflection, keeping the same low register, turning the question almost into a statement.

Something in the fevering of her pale cheeks, like droplets of Chambord blossoming in Vermouth, hints at a perpetual rage locked under those curtains of hair. There's something in its slippery darkness, its smart of freshly-poured bitumen, which claims deference. This girl

19

is conflict-polished and grit-slicked, not to be fucked with. She can't be that far from Evan's age, yet the headlamps in which he's caught tighten his jaw in apprehension. After a struggle, the hinge falls open and drops a strangled response.

"Um, nothing. Sorry."

She opens the book under her arm, removes a slim black pen from her back pocket, and begins to sketch, abstract whirls and undulating ripples, shading and blacking, biting her lower lip in concentration. He gazes back into his pint, determined to drink it steadily instead of gulping and making a break for it. She still stares at the top of his curly head. He's all too aware of his shortcomings; his riot of a hairstyle, his skinniness, his owlish eyes too large for his face. The uniform he'd taken such care to flatten and crease in all the right places is now rumpled, as a consequence of its poorly-fitted drape from his lanky shoulders, slender hips. From his peripheral vision, he watches her blurred outline lose interest in watching him, and turn back to the bar.

It's much less crowded in here now, the spectators clearly having moved elsewhere to wallow in their superiority. Probably to a place with a higher ceiling and air conditioning; the better to accommodate their nebulous, unrelenting clouds of hot air and aristocracy.

The girl exhales loudly, and slams the book closed. She leans her head on her hand, leaning further across the counter to catch the bartender's attention.

"Same again, ay, Mike, would you?" she mutters, nudging her empty glass onto the drip mat with her free hand.

The bartender, grizzled slightly by the rush of demands post-production, as well as having to chase a fucking rabbit around the bar for an hour during the show, sighs. Mike has been tending bar for as long as he's been able to sport facial hair, but the past few months on Polly's payroll have slipped past in a rash of reliably bizarre episodes that have always been best approached when flying, slightly. Tonight he'd managed to squeeze in a few solo-skinners over the duration of the play, but the debacle after the show has knocked any distance between comprehensions and comprehended into the ether. He wants to go home, preferably with Carrie. She clearly needs to talk, and this is not the place.

"Aye, hen. But have ye seen the time?" He points to an antique maritime clock looming from the top of the gantry. "It's nearly midnight. Shouldn't you be getting home by now?"

20

She idly tinkles the nail of her index finger along the row of beer taps.

"Ah, Mike. Every time you ask me that, you get the same answer. I'll roll out of here…"

"…with the last keg." He finishes for her. "I know, Carrie, but I worry about you. Doesn't your mum wonder what you're up to? Out all night?"

"Believe me, Mike, it's the last thing on her mind right now. This is infinitely better for my health than hanging around the latest episode of my mother's self-perpetuating soap opera. Just give us a Martini, would you?"

Evan holds a hand to his brow, to shield his peeking at her. He watches, fascinated, as she uncrosses her legs, stretching them to the toe-point before crossing them once more, in the other direction. She imbues each motion with such careless, incidental poetry. As though acting out a semaphore, or carrying a secret message. Her limbs simultaneously have a life of their own, yet are irrefutably hers by the measure of the grace in each ripple of movement. When Mike passes her the glass, it seeps into her being in a sleight of hand, as though anything that touched her acquired that same poetry, that second skin of light. She is scratched onto microfilm, super-imposed; so unaware of her body and its motions. The effects of her phantom flickering across the scenery in which she sits paradoxically bring about her dominance of it.

His impressionable youth kick-starts a wave of turbulence, an unfolding sequence of physical responses to which he'd never imagined he could be susceptible. Only the slow freeze-thaw of his throat, courtesy of the dwindling pint, keeps his skin together, prevents his tumbling from the stool.

That solipsistic myopia of the adolescent is called harshly into question, hauled up to the forefront of his mind and given a sound thrashing. He can't remember what he's doing here. Passage of time and space cease to register.

He forgets his name.

He has to know more.

Part II

Hilary may be about to vomit. The scent of cherry tobacco and incense is losing its clout, allowing jagged fingers of rabbit shit and tarnished coppers to poke its way up into her keen nostrils. This isn't the sole reason for her nausea. She shifts on the couch, inching further and further from Lance as Polly's hints as to what an *arrangement* might entail become increasingly overt.

"I'm afraid we don't go in for that sort of thing," her lips clip like broken castanets.

Polly sits on the opposite sofa, chubby legs tucked up under her bulk. She looks less like a tribal and more like the fucking tepee, an impression further effected by the nose and forepaws of an anaemic Pomeranian peeking out from beneath the bottom layers of her robes. She pauses to drink deep of smoke from a hookah, then,

"Sweetheart, this is the *theatre*, where anything goes. I care deeply about my customers from both sides of my…affairs, and I offer only the best of the best in return for very little."

"But you're talking about - "

"I'm saying nothing, except that it's all extraordinarily discreet. Once you've joined my inner sanctum, anything that goes on in these rooms stays in these rooms."

Polly reaches under the coffee table and produces a box, a two-handed cuboid taller than it is wide, with slanted lid like a cigarette packet. Ornate flourishes graffiti the blonde wood in burnt slashes of hybrid lettering. Tilting the lid up towards her face, she displays the contents to Hilary and Lance. They lean forward to look, desire and horror flashing across each expression in equal measure. Small packages, wrapped first in opaque white paper, then cellophane in hues of bottle green, daffodil and crimson pack the box in neat columns, arranged in traffic-light succession.

"The green ones are the starter for ten. Excellent for a jolt before a long evening in trying company. The yellow, that's for a mellower session – a slow build, a slow drop. Like floating in space."

Silence prevails, until Hilary asks the unasked question.

"And the red?"

"That's for my very, very special customers. For their own safety, and mine, there's a nonnegotiable trial period in effect before I allow them to try the red."

"So…what, exactly, are the terms again?"

"I'll tell you what. Since you've been kind enough to come to my show this evening, I'll grant a courtesy of my own. I'll give you each a taste of the yellow and green, some samples to take away and try at your leisure, before you make any decisions."

Lance nods.

"That's very kind of you, Polly."

Hilary bites her lip, before nodding herself, slowly, deliberately.

"Okay. We won't take up any more of your time. Thank you for seeing us – particularly in light of our…situation."

"There is always a way. Banknotes and coinage are simply arbitrators, a slender substitute for a lack of imagination."At this, Polly reaches into both sleeves and withdraws two tiny objects from each; bullets wrapped in the same coloured cellophane, twisted at either end like after-dinner mints. Handing Lance and Hilary a yellow and a green, she grasps their waiting hands in hers, squeezing tightly.

"I want you to think exceptionally hard about what's on offer. I may have a long client list, but each and every one is of the utmost importance to me, and I don't apportion favours lightly. I like you two; I think we'll go far."

The pair stare mutely into Polly's unctuous grin, unsure what to do next.

She releases their hands, and points to the door. They slip the nuggets out of sight; Lance into his coat pocket, Hilary into the cups of her padded brassiere.

"There's a drink waiting for each of you at the bar, if you care to stick around. As for business, it's over for the day. If you decide to go through with the deal, report to me by the end of the week. That's when the show's run is over, and this window of opportunity closes with it."

She says no more, but leans back in her seat, freeing the Pomeranian, which scuttles out from under her skirts and into her lap.

She begins to nuzzle its foxy snout, keening eerily from the front of her mouth. Dismissed, Lance and Hilary back toward the door, their eyes still on the mysterious benefactor. Once out in the hall, it swings shut of its own accord, leaving them alone with the spiders and moths in the echoing stairwell.

By the time the nervy couple arrive at the bar, the weight of Carrie's head is pushing down harder on her hand, rendering her a mass of acute angles as she falls deeper into the frazzle of the drink.

Evan has long gone. His cockiness, always tenuous at best, had faltered considerably after his second pint: drinking alone was never as much fun when he clearly lacked the panache that seemed to come so naturally to the likes of Bogart and Stewart. Nineteen and awkward, he just looked a bit pathetic. With his soft stomach feeling the worse for the whisky chaser he'd purchased, in the hope of substance backing up a lack of style, he'd shuffled off before he got too drunk to undo his cravat.

When the man with the trench coat and the woman with an apparent case of renal haemorrhoids slink into the bar, Carrie turns her face only enough to make sure they were sitting nowhere near her. They perch on stools at the bar's far end. After a few quiet words with Mike, who exhales frowzily before marking another entry in to the comps book, the pair lapse into silence with their drinks in hand.

"Mike?"

"Yes, Carrie?"

"Are you taking the night bus tonight, or a taxi?"

"Taxi. Why?"

"Ah…right. Never mind. I'm heading soon."

"I know you're fine on the bus yourself, but…wouldn't you rather stay over at mine?"

Carrie ponders this, squinting at the clock through the remnants of her martini.

"Would do, but I can't this time. Got some stuff to do tomorrow."

She's telling the truth. She has school in nine hours.

The suspension on the bus is shot to fuck, causing the framework of the vehicle to rattle to the sound and texture of incipient madness. She's forgotten why, exactly, she's bothering with school. She could be at Mike's right now, slurping hot chocolate and maybe a couple of Valium for good measure.

Some digging in the rear aspect of her fogged headspace reveals a remembered threat from her guidance teacher. Something about contacting her mum if her sporadic attendance continued. This was not a worrisome prospect in and of itself – Tracy usually settled for writing a note and skelping her across the back of the leg – but that didn't preclude the latest toy-boy from chucking in his tuppence-worth. He overestimates the capabilities of his professed youth and beauty; trying to talk to her about it, *engage* with her issues. Sure, he was young once, not as long ago as Tracy, but that distance increases exponentially and unforgivably when the counsellor in question is currently fucking your mother.

Over the short yet sobering walk from the bus-stop to the house, Carrie's private seethe is interrupted, caught off guard, by the image of the skinny, awkward guy from the bar. The one she'd railed at. A glimmer of remorse beats an unexpected path through her gin-soaked solipsism. Despite efforts to the converse, she finds herself unwillingly curious as to who the figure was, and what he was doing, like her, drinking alone.

The crunching of her boots on the stony driveway crunches up the reverie, as her concern switches to getting inside and upstairs without alerting her mother. Pausing at the front door, she listens out to ascertain the degree of wakefulness in the house. The TV blares a cop-show theme tune, over which she can hear Tracy whooping, and the vague thump of stockinged feet on the hardwood flooring. Raising an eyebrow, Carrie can only assume that they've reached the evening's fecund point, cumulating in lager-soaked giggling as Kevin chases her mother around the sofa.

Easing the door on, she slips into the hall and proceeds up the stairs, sideways, two steps at a time. She exhales loudly as she steps into her bedroom, flinging her jacket and bag on the bad before following in its wake, face down, eyes closed. After a minute's pause, listening out for any acknowledgement of her covert entry, she turns over, sits up and rummages in the top drawer of her bedside cabinet. She discovers a handful of jelly babies in a crumpled wrapper, and devours them idly, though still in order of colour, before coming upon her real quarry. A plastic bubble, which once held the prize from inside a Kinder Egg, now rattles with a different kind of promise. Shucking the halves apart, she shakes out a handful of azure capsules into her hand. With her free hand, she sets the alarm on the digital clock on the tabletop, and then claps her other palm to her mouth. Despite being dry-swallowed, the Seroquel hits her gut with satisfactory haste, melting into the foundations laid by the rest of the evening's intake. Getting undressed, she's a date rapist's fantasy, performing a wall-eyed striptease adorned with the rapturous half-smile of the sleepwalker. Safe in the knowledge that no occupant of the house dared enter her bedroom without prior permission, she collapses, on top of the duvet, clad only in the swollen satisfaction of another night well-spent.

Evan has never been more relieved to skip a third-degree upon rolling home late and half-cut. It has less to do with his mum's disapproval, and more to do with feeling like an absolute tit, without being able to figure out why. Aside from the obvious, which he'd resigned himself to long ago.

He hangs up his jacket carefully on the coat-rack, then sits on the bottom step to remove his black winkle-pickers. Despite his care, the slickness hasn't held up – they're now dusty and scuffed, looking as battered as he feels. He leaves them in the hall, and, as an afterthought, tucks the cravat into the jacket pocket. By leaving these articles of clothing outside of his bedroom, their reproach can be somewhat diminished for the time being.

All things considered, he tells himself, in that balmy life-coach tone of voice he's inherited from his mother, the evening had been a success. He has a job now, and easy one, with undeniable perks. He's just disappointed that the lifestyle hadn't fallen into his lusty lap.

Slowly, he boxes each sepia cell of the daguerreotype flitting across his internal projector. No moustachioed beatniks with records under their arms. No prettily plump whores with hearts of gold. No cocktail shakers undulating through fragrant air, shearing bolts of silver light across the faces of the watching punters. No thespians slaking their thirst at the bar after an onstage explosion of erotic excess. No famous faces or drolly delivered anecdotes with which to impress the guys at university the next day. No fucking *tips*, either. All childishly fatuous; and all a clear indication that he ought to work harder to rein in any tendencies toward inhibition and conceit. That girl at the bar had called him on it, pinning his ego firmly to the floor like a lepidopterist skewering a butterfly.

But no matter. To bed, to sleep, to dream no more.

26

Hilary's heel clatters against a metal post, the sign at the top of which proclaims *Taxi Rank*. The evening has not gone according to plan. This is not the way thinks usually work out – when she finds herself in financial, legal, administrative, narcotic, sexual, or spiritual trouble, something always comes through. Something *just right,* to melt on her tongue and through her being like a sherbet fountain, bending to the command of her coquetry and gleaming teeth. She was accustomed to getting her own way; this arrangement is so entirely under the authority of another that she feels like a pant-wetting schoolgirl hauled to the school nurse for a scolding, and a loan of someone else's knickers. All Lance's fault, she decides. Smug little shit.

"I hate you," she growls, without taking her eyes from the middle distance awaiting the sight of an available cab.

"It's extremely fortunate for us both, then, that the sentiment is more than reciprocated, dearest sister of mine."

"Half-sister. You're a substandard rendering of my father's mediocre genes. Don't dare forget it."

Lance glares at the back of her head, summoning from the depths of his overcoat an argument of adequate pomposity.

"Dear, I'm more than happy to make my own way, without impinging on your lofty ideals. You can go out there on your own, if you like. I'm not short of contacts, and I refuse to be insulted for the sake of doing you a favour."

"Come off it. You heard her; it's both of us or nothing at all."

"I can't make up my mind which is worse."

Polly reclines most pleasantly in the arms of a down-engorged lounger. Although she hasn't put pen to paper over the course of the day, she luxuriates in the surety of all the verbal contracts…casual as they seemed, on such matters they were anything but tenuous. She opens a box of imported liqueur chocolates. Placing one on the tip of her tongue, she presses it against her hard palate, the better to delight in the slow melt. It tastes like power, the sweetness of the cocoa butter enveloping the tang, the levelling pinch of brandy. She smacks her lips into a grotesque protrusion, a wicked smirk seated firmly in the knowledge that there would be some worthwhile additions to the upcoming shows.

Wrestling an arm over her swaddled mass, she reaches to the floor for a remote control. Pointing it at the television screen, she presses *play*. Her entire being lights up with the screen and its joyous revisiting of previous success. As figures begin to move within the image, she superimposes the faces of Hilary and Lance. She hadn't lied – she *did* like them – but less for their questionable amiability, and more for the potential trapped within those still-lithe bodies, echoing around those vacuous heads. They may neither be decided nor enthused about the performance to come, but, as she knows by now, *that's entertainment.*

Part III

Hilary has been staring at the same paragraph for the past half hour. It hangs in suspension on the computer screen before her, the words and characters obstinately refusing to resolve themselves into any kind of sense.

She can't concentrate because the two little nodules of escape, locked in the top drawer of her desk, are squeaking out for attention. The temptation to just fucking *go for it* and be done with it is giving her a stomach-ache, but she's afraid. Something in Polly's delivery implies a promise that's going to hurt to keep. That there's something special about this stuff that's going to keep her coming back. That, perhaps, no subsequent hit will ever be the same. With the addicts' intolerance of the permanent fixture, she loathes the idea of being chained to a deal almost as much as she loathes being strung out at her desk on a weekday morning, where time refuses to move and neither knowledge nor inspiration have bothered to show up to work.

Although in advertising there's a certain amount of leeway granted for creativity to manifest itself, there does come a point whereby an utter dearth of output attracts negative attention. Blank screens and silence have yet to have made an impression on even the most lateral-thinking consumer. Going by the subject line in the email, she's supposed to be pitching an advert for laundry detergent, but instead of tackling stubborn stains, her mind is engrossed in a nosebag of possibilities. Housewives in floral pinafores cavort through Elysian fields of purest white, but the powder in question is certainly not of the lemon-scented variety.

Cathy, her secretary, sticks her head around the office door, giving Hilary such a start that she thumps her knee painfully off the underside of the desk.

"Ms Carntyne? I have your brother on line one."

Swallowing a venomous stream of invective, Hilary rubs the developing bruise and forces a smile.

"Thank you, Cathy. Just patch him through, I'll take it in here."

"Will do, Ms Carntyne."

"Oh, and Cathy? Shut the door behind you, would you?"

"Yes, Ms Carntyne."

The eager-beaver school-leaver hadn't seemed to tire yet of the repetition of Hilary's name, or of rolling the office lingo around her dentist's scaffold of a mouth. She even picked her coffees to stretch as many syllables out of the specifications as possible, with her half-fat, light-foam, double-tall, extra-hot, gingerbread-syrup mochacchino. With whipped cream, chocolate sprinkles and fucking *marshmallows* on top, of course. Hilary had taken to sending her on long, pointless errands, to hunt for non-existent documents and imaginary stationery items, just to get her away from the office for as long as possible. Or to see if she'd cry – that was good, too.

Ah, but here came the conversation with dearest Lance. The green light flashing on the telephone looked too much like her other alert-system for comfort. Picking up, she drawls,

"Good morning, dear heart. And how does the day find my brother?"

"Hilary, sweetness: anything you're doing, drop it right now. You have to come over. You have to give this a shot. I can't say much more."

"Let me guess. You've decided to open Polly's bag of tricks. Brave boy."

"Leave now, you can rake me over when you get here."

Hilary closes her eyes for a moment. When she opens them, that stupid piece of copy is still taunting her from the screen. This wasn't working. She had to give something else a shot, in the interests of research. Expanding the mind.

"I'll be right over. I just gotta get somebody to cover me."

Hilary smiles evilly, and pushes the intercom. Cathy answers, and, before she can slip her bosses' name silkily through the wires, Hilary cuts in.

"Cathy, get in here."

The Lacoste-slippered Grail-seeker enters as though in anticipation of forty lashes, then relaxes when she sees Hilary's grin.

"Cathy, you've learned a great deal over the past few months. I know you're passionate about advertising as a career. So I've decided to give you a little more responsibility. Do you think you're ready for it?"

"Oh! Yes!" she cries, in the throes of a clerical orgasm. "Oh, Ms Carntyne, I've had the best of examples, watching you work. I shall do the very best I can, I'm sure I can manage!"

Hilary squeezes her legs, buttocks, teeth and stomach muscles together, holding in a shriek of laughter. Give her a few years in the business and she'd certainly have that enthusiasm torn a new hole. Now all that remained was to find the girl something to keep her occupied, and clock enough of Hilary's computer time to imply the ongoing of a day's work.

"Right. See this batch of documents? I want you to go through every brand mentioned, and look up their advertising campaigns from the past five years. Then summarize them, chasing them up with the sales figures that followed each campaign. Can you manage that?"

Cathy's expression, befitting that of a healed cripple chucking aside her crutches, answered the question. Fuck, if Hilary was lucky, she'd come back tomorrow to enough material to take the rest of the week off.

"Other than that, just the usual. Take calls. Keep the place tidy. If anybody phones for me, I'm at a pharmaceuticals convention for the day. Tell them to call back tomorrow."

"Thank you ever so much, Ms Carntyne. I won't let you down."

Hilary feels rather pleasant about the whole thing now, practically a Miss Jean Brodie.

Shit, she had to get the stuff out of the drawer. The weeping sea-cucumber of a secretary still stood behind the desk, waiting, probably, to slip in and get comfortable in the warmth of Hilary's departed rear.

"Here," Hilary hands Cathy a tenner. "Since you're in charge, you can send someone else for the coffee. Although it's polite to ask the rest of the girls if they'd like something, don't you think?"

"Oh. Of course, yes, I'll start with that."

She surfs away on her dream-wave, leaving Hilary alone to unearth her other little helpers. This had better be good. She wasn't looking forward to the upsurge in obsequy that would no doubt follow this experiment in delegation.

Gathering her belonging into a neat leather briefcase, she scans the office for anything else that may be of use tomorrow morning, when she'd have to counter her brief sensory vacation. Seeing nothing that resemble a church bell, a cattle prod or a forklift, she brushes off the cloying dust of public opinion. Satisfied with a well-executed decision, she sweeps herself out of the office and unofficially off the planet.

Lance lives on the outskirts of the city, in an archipelago of self-involved cul-de-sacs whose version of community spirit boils down to building higher walls instead of erecting electric fences. This suits him perfectly. After the split with the last of his high-maintenance girlfriends, he'd come to the realisation that he enjoyed his own space far too much to share it with an endless array of pose-able dolls. Not only did they take liberties with his stash – he could deal with that, he had the money – but they unfortunately came unequipped with options to mute or refrain from talking about how they planned to spend his money.

Tahina had had potential – he'd begun to tune in occasionally whenever she chirped strings of numbers over the unfurled pages of wedding magazines and cruise brochures. A build-up of tolerance had begun; he stopped noticing the streaks of St Tropez streaking the bed, the towels, the settee. He no longer asked what she'd bought when she placed his card on the telephone table. He hadn't minded when she'd begun to grow a slight paunch – no doubt as a result of her now unlimited access to Lance's heaving fridge and wine cellar.

Only when she'd totalled his Bentley did he realise the lengths and breadth of this slow, insidious castration. Amid the sheared strips of scarlet steel, hunched between the popcorn crumbs of twisted metal, there lurked an omen of more to come, and worse. This wasn't helped by the saucy glances exchanged between Tahina and the thighs-for-biceps mechanic who'd brought her back. He began to see the relationship for what it really was – a parasite-host co-dependency, albeit with better shoes. His whole home, tainted, his autonomy called severely into question. Worst of all, he couldn't even claim a broken heart, so inured was he to the same stretched faces and the same trash-magazine-generated streams of *wank* issuing from the same girls' surgically-enhanced pouts. He had had enough of the conveyor belts. He was getting too old for truffle-rooting.

He'd sold his bachelor pad. There was too much light, too many mirrors, too many flat surfaces ringing back his solitude to him in mocking echo. Uprooting to the suburbs had generated a great deal of ridicule from his colleagues at the bank, who lamented the convenience of swinging past the flat of a coffee break. Therein lay the upside: if they couldn't be bothered traipsing all the way out to Pandora Court after work, the frequency of their stash-plundering visits would be diminished.

And now the airy palace of self is Lance's, and his alone. He sees no irony in the purchase of meals-for-one, he revels in the surplus of coffee left in the percolator after he's had his morning gallon, he farts and belches and scratches his backside with riotous aplomb.

He lets rip one last emission before Hilary arrives. He stands, in boxers and a t-shirt, in the bay window peering from between the tightly-pulled curtains, squinting at the front lawn.

When the white Audi pulls into the driveway, his lower legs begin a hearty jig rivalled in enthusiasm only by the copious saliva gathering between cheek and gum. She stalks up the path looking a little frayed around the mouth and eyes, probably a consequence of some tooth-grinding over the course of a sleepless night. Lance bolts for the front door, opening it a crack as Hilary mounts the front step.

"Quick, get inside."

He grabs her by the wrist and hustles her into the hall, before slamming the door and throwing closed the locks. The lounge is set up with low-burning candles and a couple of ottomans wrapped around a coffee table. The blackout pervades throughout the house; even the skylight over the staircase is lined with calico.

"What the fuck, Lance, you raising the dead or something?"

"Not quite, although it does require an equally open mind, dear. This set-up is merely the cherry on top. Did you bring yours?"

"Yeah. But before that, two things. First of all, I want to know if you fully understand the ramifications of what you've entered into. Second, put some fucking clothes on."

Lance reaches for the arm of the couch, from which he grabs a satin bathrobe of twilight blue. Throwing his arms into it, tying the belt with a flourish, he responds,

"The answer to your question, and more besides, can be found in these packets. Simply put…it doesn't matter anymore."

Carrie's guidance teacher is also the head of the prom committee, thus receives a double-barrelled blow from her charge's derision for both academics and school spirit.

Mrs Halliday is rarely brought to her wit's end – teaching in Glasgow tends to up the barometer in terms of tolerating anti-social behaviour. However, she still finds herself rocking in frustration each and every time Carrie leaves her office after yet another bollocking. She can't understand why such a smart kid refuses to thrive in the scholastic environment. She's only there by default, taking superfluous advanced Highers, in the absence of anywhere else to put her, and as a consequence of her undeniable, albeit hidden, genius. It's almost as though some other pupil had shown up to the examination hall to acquire for Carrie those faultless grades. These achievements are about the only thing keeping her in school – if the criteria were marked solely in terms of attendance and attitude, she'd have been out on her rear long ago.

This afternoon's meeting with Carrie began in the usual fashion, with Carrie's sulky refusal of tea and biscuits, and monosyllabic responses to questions. Mrs Halliday ditched the preliminaries and barrelled in.

"Carrie. We've gone around and around this more often than I care to enumerate. Turning up to class is certainly progress, I can't deny that, but it doesn't make too much difference if you forever insist on causing such a...*ruckus.*"

Carrie smiles, flatly. She's a bit rough today, and being of the opinion that nothing shook off the fuzz of an evening's excess better than an argument, she'd started with her chemistry teacher.

Mr Connor had made the mistake of bringing up the mining industry as a topical lead-on to talking about the use and misuse of fossil fuels. Carrie had taken the opportunity to whip up a feverish debate centred in her grasp of socialism and green party politics, and its intended annihilation of the monstrous Tory predilections brewing in parliament. Just to see what would happen. The rowdier class members had joined in with gusto, simmering the debate down into a vigorous critique of the school's popularity pyramids as a reflection of society as a whole. It was all smoke and mirrors – argument for its own sake – but poor Mr Connor was once more reduced to weeping quietly into his coffee mug as the dispute roared on.

Everything that came from Carrie's lips was unrehearsed, unsubstantiated and completely irrelevant, yet never once slipped out of the realm of the maniacally cerebral. Carrie does this often, more for her own amusement than with any grand manifesto to undermine the authority of the powers that be. It helps that, in spite of its Catholic persuasion, Corpus Christi High School is of a painfully conservative bent, leaving much prospect for inciting rebellion.

"Sorry, Mrs Halliday. I only mentioned a couple of things I'd read about Thatcherism. I thought Mr Connor would have been interested."

Mrs Halliday shakes her cotton-wool helmet in despair.

"Carrie, any more of this and I can't let you go to the Prom. I don't want to have to resort to pulling rank, here. There's only a few months to go before you're finished with school – can't you keep a lid on it until then?"

"Gee, Mrs Halliday, I'm sorry. I think my heart would break into little pieces if I couldn't go to the Prom! That's the kind of thing that would follow me around for the rest of my *life*!"

Mrs Halliday is no stranger to sarcasm, but the thought of cracking open yet another argument looks about as attractive as supervising detention for the rest of the year. She lets it go, and settles for a spot of bribery.

"Okay. I'll tell you what. I know you're a favourite in the Art department: at least, I haven't had any complaints from Mr Hooker. I'll have a word with your other teachers. As long as you're signed in first thing in the morning, I'll arrange it so that you can spend as much time as you like in the studio. That way, any time you feel a need to *express* yourself, you can head on over to Hooker's classroom and get it out of your system. Does that sound fair enough?"

Carrie thinks this over. Competition for space and materials in the scandalously small and ill-equipped art department was pretty heavy. Having free and easy access to the rooms would be a great way to get the jump on both her school projects and those of her own that she never seemed to have time for.

"So….what you're saying is…if I show up for registration, I can spend the rest of the day in art class?"

Registration wouldn't pose too much of a problem. Corpus Christi hasn't yet caught up with the rest of the planet and implemented an electronic system; instead, it relies on hand-delivery to the office of roll-calls from each class. She'll have a word with one of the hash-heads, offer him a cut from her next shipment in exchange for signing her in any mornings she fails to show.

"I do expect you to turn up on occasion to your other classes. I thought having the option whenever you're feeling particularly verbose might help calm things down. But, essentially, if you're on school property as and when you should be, and if your grades in your other subjects don't suffer, I don't have a problem with that."

Mrs Halliday can already hear the sound of jungle drums; if the school board got wind of this arrangement, she'd be in trouble. But, it was either this, or a footing the bill for psychiatric treatments from the teachers increasingly on the brink of insanity, trying to deal with Carrie's tirelessly inventive anarchy.

"Cool. Thanks, Mrs T. I appreciate that. I really do, I'm not being, y'know, *wide.*"

"I know you'll do what you have to. How are things at home? I haven't heard from your mum in a while."

Carrie's smile crumples into a bitter pretzel.

"Same. Happy families and all that. But I deal."

"Just…remember that you can come and talk to me anytime. I lost my own father when I was about your age, and I know how hard it can be sometimes."

"My old man didn't die. My mum just says he's dead – it's the only way she can keep face. He fucked off because he couldn't stand the sight of us."

"Oh, Carrie, you know that's not true. People do all sorts of things for all sorts of reasons. You can't blame yourself."

"I don't. I blame whoever or whatever caught his eye, and seemed a more attractive proposition. Can I go now?"

Mrs Halliday rests her chin in her palm, taking one last look at the lost girl in the plastic chair. Fighting the urge to plumb her repertoire for platitudes, which she suspects Carrie holds in contempt, she exhales an ineffectual breath and gestures to the door.

"Yes, Carrie. Be good, now. You have so much potential."

"Will co, Mrs T. Catch you later."

Carrie feels a bit rotten on her way out of the administration block – she likes Mrs Halliday, if only for the fact that she actually speaks to her now and then.

The studio access was a fucking prize, too. She'd sleep there if she thought she could get away with it, but hey, this was almost as good.

It's too late now to head over there – the meeting with Mrs T has taken up most of the afternoon, and the last classes of the day were finished with. Tomorrow would be a different story, but for now there's no other option but to head home.

By the time she's in her bedroom, kicking off her boots and tearing elastics from her hair, she's already got plans for the next couple of pieces. She's going to paint some thinly-veiled caricatures of the most popular kids, unflattering ones, and place them in situations of awkward compromise. Maybe get some collage going in the background, and some captions…fun and games. She toys with the idea of going out again this evening, but decides to try again with the whole decent-pupil thing, as a favour to Mrs T. The resolve lasts well into the early evening, as she flicks through her textbooks, highlighting passages of interest.

Then Tracy comes home, with a bang, which may indicate a brewing storm. Tracy works as a dental receptionist in the city. For a gig that requires little more than punctuality, basic literacy and numerical skills, she often came home complaining of symptoms of stress, that modern malady. She suffers tremors, headache, nausea, cold sweats and a myriad of other complaints, ostensibly brought on by the staggering amount of broken mouths seeking repair. Carrie holds back from informing her mother that these symptoms may have more to do with the amount of cheap wine and lager she puts away of an evening – that would imply that Carrie herself knows anything about struggling through the day's activities under the fog of a crippling hangover.

She hasn't seen Tracy for more than a fleeting adieu since Monday. A single tread pounding along the ground floor, the chink of a wine bottle on the counter instead of the tinny patter of beer cans, would indicate that she's alone, at least for now. It's probably as good a time as any to shoot the breeze, and maybe elicit some cash.

Plastering a smile across her face, the better to display the commendable results of all those railway sidings and rubber bands, Carrie descends to the sitting room.

"Hi, mum."

Tracy doesn't reply so much as jerk her head vaguely in Carrie's direction. It must have been a bad day, right enough – her blonde beehive now a veritable hornets' nest, her face of make-up about an inch further down than the level required for the intended effect. She sits slumped in the armchair with one arm resting on her plump stomach, clutching a glass of red close to her armpit, the quicker to reach her mouth. In the other she holds a remote control, at which she stares as if examining an asteroid freshly fallen from the sky. She looks a lot older than the twenty-eight she's going for (always erring on the side of caution, stripping a mere seven years from her real age), and more preoccupied than usual, if such a thing were possible.

"Mum? How's things?"

An hour passes, or so it seems, before Tracy turns to face her daughter.

"Hello, Carrie. I'm fine! I mean, everything's grand. I mean…where have you been?"

"School."

"No – this week. I haven't seen you for ages."

Carrie hesitates before explaining her whereabouts. Tracy was pretty easy-going about most things, but depending on her mood, mentioning the theatre sometimes tore open seams of jealousy. There had been more than a few bones of contention passing between Tracy and her mother-in-law: Zinnia had accused Tracy of ensnaring her boy, of bleaching the art from his bones. To a degree, she'd been right. Frank's disappearance had no doubt appealed to Zinnia's taste for the absurd, had the trick not left her granddaughter without a father. His failure to emerge from the starry chamber with a bouquet of sparklers left Zinnia at a loss as to her place in the family. Because she'd never patched things up with Tracy, her gift to Carrie could be interpreted as either a heartfelt peace offering, or a silent bird-flip from beyond the grave.

"Nowhere special. Just kicking about in town."

The corners of Tracy's mouth spread without any discernable degree of elevation, utilising three of the four muscles apparently required to smile.

"You've been at the theatre."

This isn't a question.

"Well, yeah. Polly has a new play running. I thought I'd check it out."

Tracy sighs. At least, she supposes, it's something cultural.

"Just…make sure you're careful. Some freaky folks out at night. And that you get some dinner. You're getting awfully skinny."

Carrie forces down yet more statements of the obvious; that there's nothing but wine in the fridge, and that she's been prowling the streets late at night since she was old enough to hop on the bus without a chaperone. Kevin's absence this evening has clearly opened a wedge in her mother's perception of the surrounding environment: she's remembered she has a daughter.

"Sure, mum. I will."

Tracy's eyes light up as she grasps hold of another potential avenue of conversation.

"How's school these days? You must be behaving; I haven't heard from that bloody Halliday woman for a while."

"It's still there. I'm still there. That's about all."

"Right. Long as you're keeping your nose clean."

Tracy has run out of things to ask. Her mental checklist of Things A Mother Should Know is satisfactorily completed, and now Carrie turns right back into an avatar, a doppelganger, a lodger. Yet she continues to stand there. She must be after something.

"Erm...you away out tonight? I mean, you alright for money?"

The deal is done. Any remaining threads of Carrie's resolve to stay at home effervesce at the prospect of the alternative...yet more stilted questions and painfully feigned interest.

"A few quid wouldn't hurt, if you can spare it."

Tracy has her mind set on an evening's wine-sodden self-pity and reality television. It was more difficult to feel superior to the fat sots on the diet programmes or the Burberry-clad smackheads with Carrie hanging about, reminding her of her own shortcomings. A handout was a small price to pay for a few hours worth of increasingly sloppy channel-surfing. She places the glass on the side table, roots around in her purse, and, without counting it, hands her daughter a fetid wad of cash.

"There you go. Get a lift home off that nice barman. He seems like a decent sort."

"I won't be home. I'm staying over at a mate's. I'll be back tomorrow."

Even better. Tracy can now safely fall asleep on the couch. Nothing took the pleasure out of a few beverages than that hasty scuffle toward bed, brushing teeth, arranging pajamas, remembering to lock the door...if Carrie wasn't coming home, all she'd have to worry about was setting her alarm for the following morning.

Carrie pockets the cash, then thunders upstairs for her boots, bag, jacket and sketchbook. Good intentions still push at the edges; she figures she'll do a few pencil studies in preparation for her new projects.

She wonders why her mother is so pliable this evening. Perhaps she's had a fight with Kevin. These apocalyptic brawls were doubly disturbing – the thump of wood on bone, glass on concrete, the floor-shaking cacophony of both shrieking to break the sound barrier...this was nothing. What really turned the stomach was the inevitable squeaking and yelping and ululating that played out over the reconciliation sex. Carrie preferred to skip these particular concertos, relocating to the theatre where the hallucinatory goings-on were bracketed by dusty velvet.

She doesn't bother, this time, with even a perfunctory glance at the mirror. She'd had a shower that morning, that would have to do. Afraid of any further expansion of her mother's conversational repertoire, she trips downstairs as softly as possible. Then out, out into that good night before the equilibrium could be further disturbed.

Evan wakes in the early afternoon, which, unlike his ilk as bemoaned by parents nationwide, is not a frequent occurrence. Still burrowed fixedly under the duvet, he presses the light function on his wristwatch. One-thirty bathes him in a soft green glow, gently informing him that he'd missed his morning lecture. *Shit.*

Resigned, he takes his time unfurling. Going by the tangled shroud of the top-sheet enveloping him from the waist down, the pillows slumped at the wrong end of the bed, and what feels like a nasty bruise on his cheekbone roughly the shape of the edge of the bedside cabinet, he's had a restless sleep.

Peeling his head, slowly, he takes in the low-lit chaos of his bedroom. A Matisse composition of disparate elements glowers from before his desk. A chair robed in a shirt and tuxedo jacket, shoes lined up underneath, trousers draping from the seat to the floor with a pint glass of water resting on the crotch, all impart the illusion of the a skinny orchestra conductor watching from the edge of the room. His mother must have brought them up this morning, no doubt shaking her head at the noxious alcoholic emissions unfurling from his sopoforic form.

Evan sits up, delicately grasping his head. He has hours to go before he's back for his second shift, and he can't fight through the shutter-click of images racing across his mind. He's reminded of an acquaintance's description of the effects of acute jet-lag, brought on by chasing the sunlight for three weeks across Singapore, New York, Bangkok, Amsterdam, and Dubrovnik in an order of no discernable logic.

"Mate, you start to *see* shit. All the languages start to sound like Gaelic. Or Dalek. The heads move from body to body, y'know: like little Thai waitresses start to look like Jewish shopkeepers. The fellas in the hash cafés all look like Ivan The Terrible. Then you get scared to leave the hotel in case you get lost and wind up in fucking *Narnia*. Crazy stuff, man, crazy stuff."

Craig had been onto something, there, that fit the bill. Evan reconciles himself to the fact that messing with folk's heads is probably Polly's remit: that if anyone leaves her theatre without the vaguest frisson of disturbance, she's feel like she hadn't done her job properly. Although...it isn't so much the show that's dropping strips of warped celluloid along the bottom of his skull. It's the solidly intense atmosphere thereafter. The performers had disappeared backstage without a hint of re-appearance, later on, in their civilian garb. Only Polly herself had swept through the crowd, absorbing thanks and praise. And she hadn't stuck around for too long, herself, leaving the punters to mill around without any clearer picture of what the hell that *was*. The show had been like a guerrilla attack; violent, unapologetic, allowing the onlookers to formulate their own deductions as to the agenda. A production within a production, a full-on, bits-out theatrical experience, right enough. He's trying to fool himself into thinking there's not another image floating up at the ceiling, drifting like a kite string with ribbons of knotted drinking straws. That girl, the rude one with the torn denims and the dirty boots – she's still there, growling like a wildcat, mocking his hair, his clothes, his unpractised necking of a shot of whisky and the subsequent ghosts of tears pushing at his eyelids. He can still taste it, melding with the turgid blowback of mortification.

Right, it's time to make some headway on the day. He wrestles out of bed and promptly stands in a water glass, thankfully plastic this time, and wobbles comically before regaining his centre of balance. Tiptoeing between stacks of messy ring-binders and ragged textbooks, he throws a dressing gown over his boxer shorts and makes his way downstairs. His mother isn't home, going by the empty hooks on the coat-stand and key-shelf, but she's made her presence felt. The whole ground floor reeks of furniture polish and cinnamon buns. There's a place set for one at the kitchen table. Cold toast hardens disapprovingly in the rack between pots of jam and honey, a pitcher of apple juice diluted by long-melted ice. All are lit up in a stream of blistering sunlight, admonishing him for his idleness.

He sets the kettle to boil, and tips enough coffee and sugar into a mug to turn the resultant mixture into molasses. With this he sits and stares from the window, into the garden, willing the melting, separating elements from the night before to resolve into a comprehensible narrative.

Nothing will make sense until this evening. In spite of his cultivation of the creative, he's still a great believer in formulae, in the mathematics to be found in even the most obscure circumstances. Growing up under his mother's tutelage has given him a reliable set of rules, codes of conduct and propriety with which to handle anything, even the sinking of a ship or an imminent nuclear explosion. Together they'd handled his father's desertion, the attendant questions and the suddenly awkward footnotes required in filling out tax returns. After that horror show of embarrassment, straddling the as-yet undefined customs of the theatre would be child's play.

Part IV

Whilst Evan wraps his lips around a succession of tooth-melting coffees, an uplift of a different nature is in its first heat, over in Pandora Court.

It all happens in seconds. No watch-checking, no glances between the two to compare effects, just instant flight, atomic boom. Everything on the floor relocates to the ceiling, most noticeably Hilary herself, pressed against a enclosure without substance, the only thing keeping her from flying out and up into the sky. Everything on the ceiling paves the floor, as the firmament throws off its graces and joins the worshippers.

The room itself begins to take on the geometry of the inside of a marquee, bulbous and tapering at the top as the candle flames swell and recede from the edges of her vision. She more than sees the stars: she feels them, as Orion himself dismounts from his inky backboard and envelops her in a searing kiss.

Lance pounces in his tiger's pelt, chasing woodland animals around the room. He roars a feedback of synth in stereo, louder than a train wreck and with a crunch born of bloodlust. He finds a space on the floor with adequate room to turn around with arms outspread, at which point he drops and curls into a ball of glee, sliding around on a puddle of (thoughtfully-scented) nut butter which has momentarily replaced a buff-coloured throw cushion.

Hilary leaves, jumps into her car, drives to the edge of a nonexistent canyon and launches herself from the lip, screaming and clutching at comet tails all the way down. All from her perch on the edge of the ottoman.

The noise is immense as each and every sonic particle from both minds conjoin, intermingle into a melody both glorious and appalling. Forests of tone grow up around bramble patches of chord and note.

43

Two bodies at once fill the space and shrink to infinitesimal dimensions, touching and untouchable, skins flayed to the senses. Their experiences are disparate yet irrefutably conjoined; they communicate without speaking. Neither has the words, if they could: nothing is static or coherent enough to bow to the logical constraints of mere language. The drug has taken them outside the reach of points of articulation, annihilating any uprising syllables within the very chamber of the salivating mouth.

Half an hour has passed, in which they've already travelled far beyond the parameters of a paltry three dimensions, defying time, space, gravity, genus and instinct. Doorways are no longer wood and paint, but avenues of escape and discovery, onto vast expanses of ripened understanding that nothing can be understood. They circle an earth laid bare, bisected like a cored apple, open for exploration.

This interlude is just the beginning, literally the green light, on what's to follow.

Hilary peels herself from the ceiling and rubs the edge of her palms against the join between her thighs and the seat. She's still here. The room declines to resume its original dimensions entirely, however, and she's unsure when Lance's pet Siamese will cease rolling its own disembodied head about the laminate flooring.

Lance is back to his old self again, almost, stood up and peering from the crack between the curtains. He pats his coccyx absent-mindedly, checking for the tail that was recently such a marvellously amusing addition to his anatomy.

Through the tunnel of perceptions calls Hilary, having found her voice again.

"That. Was. Incredible."

Her voice, tissue-papered, whispers in awe. Lance turns and stares, searching for her name and face amid the sudden influx of new information, before replying to the echo of her voice surfacing in his memory.

"There's more. We haven't taken the yellow."

They're both silent, basking in the warmth emanating from the split in the curtains. Shadows in the room have barely moved an inch while they've been gone. The brevity of the time spent in the green has levered open an aperture of possibility into the next round…this could go on for hours. Hilary remembers her deputy, left in charge of the office, and a quiver of guilt shoots across the remainder of her high.

"What time is it?"

44

"I don't particularly care. You don't either: be honest."

Lance is right, to her irritation. Something has to be done to get rid of this inconvenient remorse. A bit of come-down chit-chat fills the gap nicely.

"What did she say about the green? A 'jolt', huh?"

Lance raises an eyebrow, pulling the corner of his mouth back in irony.

"I must admit, that had a little more of a clout than I had expected."

"Come off it; you're no amateur. So what about this yellow?"

There's a nagging intonation from her sober version of herself, crawling up onto her shoulder, hissing in her ear. Something about arrangements. Conditions. Payment. She can't think about this right now. There are more important things to be seen to – her high is well and truly dissolving now, and she can't let that happen. Not yet, not when that lush vista of rapture had only just come into view, when she's only halfway there, when the day was only half-done.

Lance duly fetches a clean tray from the kitchen, upon which rests a mirror, a saucer, a razor and a bundle of cotton buds next to a shot-glass of vodka.

"Would you like to cut, or shall I?" he asks, placing the yellow baubles on the saucer.

"Go ahead, dearest. Let's see what merriment awaits, shall we?"

Polly's words chime in again, something about floating in space. After the rampage of sensation and veritable aerobics of the previous session, the promise of buoyancy glows with insulated bliss. They begin.

Yellow. Midsection. Stamina. Coasting aircraft. Multiple orgasm. Flash. Flash. Electric angelfish of light swim across the retina. Thunderclouds appear and dissipate across the span of seconds, like a blast from a freezer door swung open, sucked shut. Air first thick, tarry, then dispersal, no encore. They ride thermals mechanized like the subway. Destination voiceover incoherent, another language, terminating unknown nowheres.

Shaking rope-bridge over torrents, flecks of mountain spring stinging eyes as they cross the delta. Watery furrows wrinkle the earth, telling tales older than civilization.

Then, back into the city, the sprawl an open mouth, screaming out a thousand electric can openers, a million feral beasts in heat. The hunt is on, the big game are ripe for the picking.

The taxis have tiny television screens now, implanted right into the back of the drivers' heads. Stop. Don't want to get out, don't want to arrive anywhere, would rather see the end of the movie…spoilsport, come out come out. Slow down, you fucking amateurs, you ingrates. Approaching a bed of daffodils, lay down to sleep, and they're nothing but a fucking ring of traffic cones.

But there's something buzzing at the limits of the impossible; the yellow marks the transition between the stop and go, keeps them bound however pleasurably in the limbo between the real and unreal. Even as the crucible of hallowed excess simmers, throwing great bubbles of light and clouds of ether into the trip, alongside runs the knowledge that it can't be maintained on its own. They need more, a top-up, pump the meniscus to the lip of the mind before they crash, and take everything else down in the wake of the broken glass. They can't come this far and leave itineraries half-finished, sentences and truths stopping dead like train tracks at the cliff's edge.

The end of the week is too far, they have to keep it going, will kill, chew powdered glass, fuck anything that moves, that gets in the way.

"Polly. We have to speak to Polly."

Evan arrives for work to find Joe in the throes of a remarkably athletic conniption fit. He thunders up and down the aisles on those swollen, nylon-wrapped black pudding legs, checking each seat number against a laminated card, even bending over his gargantuan bulk to examine the floor between the rows for litter.

Noticing Evan, he dashes up the aisle like a punctured zeppelin.

"Son, we've a bit ay a fiasco the night. That fucking bartender's rung in sick. It's just you and me oan this entire flair."
Evan ponders this briefly, before asking,

"What about Ms Monday? Isn't she always here when she has a play on?"

Joe barks a horrible chuckle.

"You think she's gonnae come down fae her tower and get her hands dirty? Nae chance. It's up tae you and me, sonny Jim. It's no gonnae   be   pretty."
This is certainly not Evan' preferred means of having his loyalty tested this early in a job. He has his doubts as to whether halving the charge

of the entire joint was entirely proportionate to taking a measure of his initiative.

"Right...so...what's the plan? Shouldn't I just do what I did last night?"

Joe's internal logic mechanisms thrum noisily as he furrows his blubbery brows. He's not a man with much endurance when it came to being on his feet: formidable slabs they may be, but they don't appreciate bearing the weight of the rest of him for any longer than is strictly necessary.

"Ahm gonnae have to...." Joe sighs, torn apart inside at having to relinquish the authority, "...leave the steward's office, and usher for the night. You're on the bar."

This arrangement is the best compromise afforded Joe: he can sit for the majority of the shift, as usual, and didn't have to worry about getting stuck behind the bar, or knocking over breakables with unmanageable lunges of his free-flowing love-handles.

Evan is less than sure.

"Em...I've never worked in a bar before."

"Aye, but you've drank in them before, aye?"

"Well, yeah, sure I have."

"Then you'll know how it goes. Just give the punters what they want, take their money, and don't drink too much yourself before half-time. Couldn't be easier."

Evan shrugs.

"I guess so."

"Good man. If wee Carrie comes by the night, she'll give you a hand."

"Who's Carrie?'

"Grand-daughter ay the dame that owned this place. Set to inherit it when she's old enough. You'll get used to seeing her about: she spends mair time here than at home."

"Okay. Anything I should know?"

Joe, mind's eye still stuck firmly between bicycle tires of his eyebrows, nods his head. The boy's fresh on the scene, right enough, but there's still risk involved in bringing him in on too much. It could go either way, particularly if Carrie's about.

"Just don't believe everything you hear. Some of the punters are a few sannies short, if you get me. Say they're fuckin' Napoleon Bonaparte if they're after a free drink."

This is a further unwanted complication. Evan knows even from his observations of the previous night that nobody seems to pay for anything at the bar, and that there must be a line drawn somewhere between gratis and taking the piss.

"Are you sure you wouldn't rather have me watch the auditorium?"

Joe shakes his jowls in refutation. He's not having the little upstart park his arse whilst Joe runs about all night.

"Naw, naw. Look, it's no that complicated. When they see a new face back there they'll know they're no in for the kind of special treatment they get aff our Mike. If they try anything with ye, just mark whatever they're after in the book. Polly'll sort it the morra. The till's usually miles down anyways, so ye cannae do much damage."

Joe claps Evan around the shoulder with a meaty palm, shunting him from the auditorium out into the main hall. The gargoyles leer from the rafters, abstract photo-fits of disparate facial features loom from between gilded picture frames. The building heaves with eyes, with watchers watching observers viewing bystanders spying on spectators. It's dizzying; he's not sure if he's up for it. Gulping back a lumpy globule of last night's whisky curd, he steps into the teak-paneled catacomb of iniquity.

Hilary and Lance don't bother with the taxi. Still wheeling, they slide into Hilary's Audi quiet certain that the white stuff hasn't any bearing on her ability to drive. After all, they now know the road, like they know every cell and pulse of the city.

They're quite correct: the car parts the traffic like a hot spoon through an ice-cream, melting the surrounding traffic into nothingness. Hilary doesn't break the speed limit – she doesn't have to – and they cruise the bisected city as they would a still lake.

The car simpers to a stop in a space that's just the right size in front of the theatre, from which they trip in elegant synchronicity up the steps. They each pause to greet their riotously attractive reflections in the glass doors, before gliding into the ambient cool of the lobby. There's nobody on the desk, yet. It's too early.

The fat steward hovers behind a small ticket booth at the auditorium entrance, having leapt from his seat at the sound of the door. Here starts the trouble.

"Good evening," begins Lance, each word a cherry blossom, a gift from his dazzling mouth. "We would very much like to see the proprietress, as soon as possible."

Joe is, to the misfortune of the radiant pair, less than keen to co-operate. He's having a hard enough day as it is, trying to keep the damn theatre from imploding under the weight of the sudden staff shortage. He's not in the mood for couriering messages in service of Polly's less reputable pursuits. Not up all those fucking stairs. No way.

"Eh...she's no about the theatre the now, you'll have to wait until after the show."

"Sir, you misunderstand me. We're here on a matter of some importance."

"I know what you're here for, and it's nothing to do with me. You'd have to speak to Ms Monday herself, and as you can see, she's no here."

Hilary leans forward, placing her perfect manicure upon the steward's flaccid jaw. She runs a fore-nail along the pitted flesh, and coos from her most sanguine roll of syllables,

"I don't know who, exactly, you think you're talking to. But we mean business, here. Do not fuck with us."

His mouth contracts to a wrinkled button-hole, at which point Lance realizes Hilary has a strangle-hold in the blubber-packed crotch of the steward's suit trousers. Her elbows scissor into a painfully acute angle as she pulls up, garroting the fly's contents with its zipper. He yowls into the front of his mouth, tears gathering in the puckered folds of his eyes. Hilary jerks, and releases her grip. The man is thrice her size, yet he cowers before her, crying like a child with an empty ice-cream cone. Such is the power of the yellow; veering its charges gently from the peaceably sedate to the flatly psychopathic. Lance reaches into the hidden depths of his coat, detaches a crisp £20 note from his money-clip and tucks it into the quivering steward's breast pocket.

"Now, I think we understand each other, don't we? My sister doesn't mince her words, I'm afraid. We are here," he repeats, "To see the proprietress. Kindly fetch her, or point us in the right direction."

Joe summons a movement from his churning gut, and with remarkable effort, replies.

"Upstairs; through that door. Knock five times."

"Thank you, sir. It's been a pleasure."

With that, Hilary and Lance retrace their steps from the previous evening, making for the door. Joe, dragging his eyeballs around the room, crumples to his knees. Hiding his head behind the booth, he moans fitfully into the heartless floorboards, lamenting the days of swagger sticks and planning a hard revenge on that fucking barman. If it weren't for the thought of what she knew, what she could do, he'd have been long gone. But that was the thing about working for Polly: you don't stay for the money or the pleasure, or for the lack of anything else to do. You stay because she has you hooked into one or more of the many strands of her empire, where every turn for the better requires an inquisition from a Sphinx, too many unanswerable questions, too many inalterable truths.

Part V

Carrie hates riding the bus under any circumstances, but the displeasure of this evening's jaunt is compounded by her relative sobriety. All the colors, voices, textures on the decrepit vehicle grate harsher on her peeled senses, without the padding of a preliminary joint. Upon alighting, she skips the shops and head straight to the theatre. Clutching her head to still the echoes, she peers through the door, keen to avoid a blowsy exchange with Polly before she's even had a drink.

Curious. There's nobody there at all. She checks her watch: there's still an hour to go before the show starts. The punters must still be gorging themselves on pre-theatre victuals.

She steps into the lobby, wincing, even after all this time, at the lurid purple drapes bringing down the high ceiling and the flaking gold paint greasing the cornicing. The air-conditioner shuffles the scent of every shoe-tread and call of nature into a malodorous cyclone, sweeping aside the pine-fresh of the wood polish.

She makes her way across the room, tiptoeing along the strip of carpet running toward the bar in an endeavor to keep her arrival unannounced for as long as possible.

A husky groan from the auditorium entrance calls a halt to the effort. She approaches the prone figure of Joe, still hunched and wailing behind the podium like a dying manatee. Assuming the long-overdue coronary had finally shown up to take the fat man down to join the other unfortunates of his mass, she speeds up, rushes over, places her hand on his shoulder. She pulls his face from the floor. He's not dying; he's making too much fucking noise and pulling too many murderous facial expressions.

"Jesus, Joe! What the fuck happened to you?"

He sets his jaw to indicate that nothing ever happens to Joe. He's too large: all orbits around his bulk, bouncing off if coming in too close. This is his purpose and function, and he will not allow it to come into question. Willing the rage to withdraw from his exterior, he wheezes a reply, and sits up.

"Aw, nothing, hen. Decked it, that's all."

Despite himself, he likes Carrie. He's fond of her, even through his disapproval of her laissez-faire when it comes to the stock. Carrie plays on this fatherly tenderness to a certain extent, although she cares enough to throw favors his way whenever she can. This has the dual purpose of massaging her conscience, and keeps things sweet when it comes to pulling strings of her own.

"Come on then. I'll fix you a cup of tea."

Joe stands, rubbing his hips, trying to stay away from his still-tender groin. He's affronted at having been come upon in his upturned beetle pose, and swiftly charges into more important matters.

"Carrie, darlin', I appreciate that, but there's a bigger problem at hand. How'd you feel about a wee bar shift the night?"

"Erm…if you need me. How come? Where's Mike?"

"Mike's not coming in. Says he has a stomach bug. Bloody chancer."

Carrie's face falls. Mike provides what amounts to the only intelligent conversation to be found around the theatre on show nights, and she'd wanted to ask him what he thought of Tracy's sudden personality crisis, her switch to concerned-parent mode. Her night out no longer seems so sociable, even if she'd only planned to draw and chat to the barman. Worst of all, the prospect of an entire evening in Joe's company tugs at her feet, weighs down each of her vertebrae. She can only take so much unsolicited interest in her schoolwork and home-life before her civility withers helpless in waves of cloying syrup. Faux-ingenuously, she asks,

"I'm not on by myself, am I? Are you going to help?"

"Naw, naw. Yer man Evan's been put on, too. He's a wee green babe, you'll need to show him the ropes. Don't get him drunk. At least not until intermission's done with."

"Ah, Joe, don't underestimate me. I'm not remotely interested wasting my time on getting some other schmuck totaled."

"Right ye are. Anyway, could ye go through and help set up? I sent the fella in to get started, and I don't want him fucking up before we've even sold the first drink."

52

Carrie nods, with a cynicism that belies her youth. She takes one more look at the pulped steward, checking his balance. She doesn't fancy her chances against his weight, if it came down to rocking him upright again.

As she makes her way to the bar, potential dangers churn in cartoon brightness across the chasms of possibility. Disappearing into the labyrinthine depths of the wine cellar. Impact injury from dropped kegs. Hands lost to the gaping mouth of the glass-washer. Burns, scrapes, scalding, splinters, fractures...all part and parcel of the service industry, rarely benign, forever in confusion. The weedy usher had better have on his cleanest panties, because if he wasn't careful, he'd be taking it up the arse in no time.

Another latent possibility, that she might just like him well enough, remains unvoiced. Having expected another evening of relative quiet and retreat, she's being thrust into sociability. Carrie is more like her father than she cares to entertain. With a zero-tolerance policy as regards the company she prefers to keep, she's a ways to go before she learns the difficulties involved in being so selective.

Taking a deep breath, as her solitude begins to flatline; she pushes open the door, and steps into the uncertainty over the crunch of breaking glass.

It's most unpleasant. With each flight of stairs, another coating of poise freeze-thaws on the skin, cracks, melts and dribbles away. Not to the point of any real remorse, but enough to raise hackles of defense against their performance in the lobby. Hilary tries to keep it elevated, in the hope of carrying them along in the streams of hot air.

"Did you see that fat fuck's *face*?"

Lance forces a snigger, his efforts suffering from his insulation against such behavior as was standard issue in private school. He's uncomfortable in the role of the overt bully: at Mont Derives, such practices were deemed too gauche, and were eschewed in favor of anonymous blackballing and rumors without nameable instigators.

"Yes, he did look rather foolish, didn't he?"

By the time they reach the top, they're three-quarters of the way down. Stood before the mightily padlocked door, their resolves begin to wane. They stare at the entrance to the fortress, silently willing the other to begin knocking. Lance breaks first, and tickles the wood with his knuckles five times, as ordered. It's now or never. There's still enough yellow in the pair for fear of losing height to override fear of whatever Polly will demand in return.

Rumble, thump, click, slide. The locks drop off and the door spreads open wide, wide and slippery and inviting, to the realm of pleasure, both fleshly and cerebral.

Polly still wears her customary bands and bolts of silk and jersey, but this time, they gleam darkly in shades of garnet and jet. Chromatography of her face, almost, with its wax lips in pale puddle, eyes black and bin-bag-shiny. No bells, no silver threads. All patterns rely upon the movement of shadows in the peaks and troughs, all authoritative sounds come courtesy of her own inflections. She briefly holds between her teeth an expression of abject fury, before she finds their faces in her internal client record. Her mouth softens into the dapper beam of a sycophant on the verge of approval. They're a little earlier than she anticipated, but she knew they would come.

Hilary begins, gathering together the strands of her far-flung authority from the buttercup haze. Her mouth co-operates with surprising efficiency, clipping,

"We're here to finalize a deal."

"So you're quite satisfied with the samples?"

Ever the mistress of the rhetorical question. She's all show, all talk, dispensing glib utterances like pocket mints. They both nod in agreement, carefully, to minimize the effect of the slow-motion delay at work on their perception. It's one of the more disconcerting of the effects; whilst being a pleasure in less demanding circumstances, it didn't do to have ten score templates of everything unraveling whilst in the midst of a serious conversation.

"Come in. This time, there is some paperwork required. Contracts, as I'm sure you'll appreciate, denote in full the depth of the undertaking."

They nod again, still slowly.

This is some serious stuff.

Evan has his upper body submerged in the depths of the ice chest, and fails to hear Carrie's entrance. A skinny arm, shirt sleeves rolled up, flops from the chasm at regular intervals, pitching fragments of glass to the floor beneath.

Fucking idiot. He's managed to swipe a tray of wine glasses over the bar and into the fresh ice. Now he's sifting through the depths and staining everything with blood, picking out the pieces to avoid inadvertently cutting punters' throats.

Carrie rolls her eyes. Amateur, aye, but this was a fucking joke. She approaches wordlessly from behind. Evan senses a bracket of body heat curling around his own. He can't turn around, still bisected and immobile. A slender hand, charcoal-grubby, reaches over his shoulder, and switches the ice machine off at the socket. With the swift completion of the task, the presence is gone, backed off, and he can emerge.

"You'll find that a lot easier if you're not too busy experimenting with cryogenics," drawls Carrie.

Evan is more than a little tired of mortification by now. He removes himself from the freezer slowly, reluctant to face the latest individual to witness his ineptitude. The combination of nervous perspiration and the abrasive air inside the ice chest forms a patina of red and white akin to a china doll. The manic sprawl of copper commas inundating his scalp doesn't do much to redress the balance. He's a gawky anachronism barely out of his teens, and it's all down to those caramelized tangerines hauling him up by the scruff.

"Thanks," he mutters into his lapels, startled to find his jaw in working order. "I didn't think of that. I'm Evan, by the way."

He holds out a hand, wincing at the state of it. Red-raw from the cold, dotted with nicks and cuts from the broken glass. Nasty. Carrie doesn't notice, simply shakes without even wincing at the cold. After an initial full-frontal scan, she looks at him only in snapshot, preoccupied with checking the fridges and gantry for stock required.

"Carrie. How many bottles can you lift at a time? We need more of…pretty much everything from the cellar. I'll set up what we have if you fetch the rest."

She runs her name into the question, a superfluous addendum to the matter at hand.

Fuck. Straight to business, and already a question of manhood. Evan has no idea.

"A fair few, I guess. Where's the cellar?"

"Down those stairs. Don't get lost."

This is not a particularly informative instruction. One rarely gets lost intentionally; the opposite isn't much less optional. She hands him a sheet of paper, listing the intoxicants required, then turns to wipe the bar, starting at the far end. The discussion is clearly over.

Evan shoulders his embarrassment and trots down to the cellar, list in hand. He's never been an expert at talking to girls, but this was ridiculous.

Seeking, gathering and hefting the wines and spirits suits him for now. There's something satisfying in the mechanics, the clank of glass on metal, the thick gulp of bottles in their as yet untapped potential. It leaves more head-room to focus on trying *not* to focus on Carrie. He can't help catching glimpses as he kicks open the cellar door, crate in both hands. She moves still in that uncanny aura, of self-possession completely lacking in narcissism. A child's arc through the novelty of air and space, attuned and alert, yet carried entirely by her own will, her determination to bend the surroundings to her ends. Each upended wineglass, she grabs by the throat between index and middle finger, flipping it upright into a perfect center of redressed balance. She rotates the goblets around a white linen napkin six times, inside and out, then a jerk around the stem to finish. She checks the shine by holding each up to the light, instead of looking for her bulbous reflection in the orb, as is often the case. Then she strings each on the overhead racks, casually tossing each glass as though lobbing screwed-up false starts from a drawing board.

Evan loads the fridges with the final lot from downstairs. Clearing his throat of perceptible tension, he asks,

"Em, can I help? I think the stock's finished."

"No, you're alright. I'm just fannying about…there's not much else to do but wait for another batch of ice."

Ouch. She doesn't intend to stick pins in, but she can't help it sometimes. Her inability to waste words makes her a terrible liar: she says what she sees, when need be. Unless she's on a roll with an irresistible wind-up, she says nothing at all if she can avoid it.

This doesn't rid Evan of his dread of silence. Scanning the hazy annals of his knowledge of popular culture, he grasps at indefinite speech bubbles for topics of conversation. She doesn't seem like one for small talk, autopsies of the lives of the rich and quasi-famous. She'd chew it up and spit it out, little gobbets of magazine pulp pasting the walls and floors. Watching tea-time television in those weary hours after classes has served him nothing but great stinking cafeteria platters of the stuff. He curses the insidious voices, the Satsuma-hued chat-show hosts and leggy roulette spinners, the useless information slipping into a consciousness left ajar and vulnerable from fatigue. No chance, here, those movements are unlearned, nothing so oily will stick to that veneer.

She has performance in her blood. A poker-face for all occasions. Meeting her eyes is a gift, a fleeting flicker, rarely held for long. She looks over shoulders, at ceiling, and is often misinterpreted as ignorant and haughty. This isn't the case – she's keeping every window in her peripheral vision open to capturing the sublime with her artist's discrimination. She treats sight, searching, casual observation and scenes sought after as a privilege, not a right. She conserves the energies of every twitch of her optic nerve, every pixel of her retina for that which is worth the look.

Conversation always incurs the same dead air, the same run of question marks. Tracy never tires of telling her that she took three years to utter her first words. She watched and listened, collecting tones and pitches, movement of lips and tongue before stringing them together into clauses, unleashing the power of the vocal cords. All or nothing – monosyllabia paves the way for shock when she breaks her silence. Her utterances are always erudite and grandiose, without the attendant pretension typical of speechifying performers. Pitch-perfect poetry, words concentrated, distilled, nothing expendable, for the right audience.

Evan says nothing, lips still squeezed together in embarrassment, not yet recovered from cocking up the ice-machine. He will learn in time that such things amount to nothing, as ice melts, water freezes, people drink and sometimes injure themselves in the process. He idly runs a cloth back and forth across the bar-top, needlessly, over Carrie's previous efforts, wishing he was a joker or a prankster or a biker or a spy or *something, anything* that would loosen the zips of the gracelessness tightening on his every inch of flesh. Carrie helps him out.

"I'm going out for a smoke. You alright here for a few?"

Of course not. He's clueless. But anything's got to beat this silence. He's never felt so stupid – he's a smart guy, amiable, pliable, well-spoken, educated. Something's not working. It's not her gender: his mother's upbringing has instilled in him a healthy respect for women, and he spends all day among other girls at university without tripping over his tongue and scrawling his flaws in neon across all available surfaces. There's something about her though, that fucking *otherness*, that's making this more than a touch too difficult, that calls for a red flag and an anvil, a hypnotist's watch, anything to scratch through the tension.

"Yeah, I'll be fine."

Her cigarette lasts a lot longer than five minutes. By the time she's exchanged words with each of the stars in turn, it's intermission. Evan runs each limb from his body in inept strands of spaghetti as he cowers under orders barked from all sides. Carrie strides back behind the bar along a pathway of yet more broken glass, kicking larger chunks out of the way as she does so. Piles of change and empty vessels, lip-stick marked, inundate the countertop, barricading the helpless bartender into a paddock of clinking anarchy.

It's a shame that the world of comic books and action heroes flies over the heads of the discerning sophisticate. Carrie's glide into action lacks only cute captions and motion trails left behind in her wake. Clutter disappears from the bar, smashing painfully into the bottle bin. Change chinks into an empty pint glass, to be tallied later on. The customers at the bar suddenly stop shouting and start listening, partly because Carrie's flat statements require silence in order to be heard, partly because they're trying to keep up with her as she whirrs efficiency through draughts of disorder.

She is really rather beautiful; her defiance, refusal to shed a drop of sweat. A sculpture of centrifugal force, binding all action into a tight circumference. Every action and statement begins and ends as it should, instead of reeling away in the wake of their vigor. Evan watches her hands around pint glasses, pushing taps and easing corks from bottles – there is no strain, no whiteness of knuckle, no shadows of jawbone to betray gritted teeth. Following her lead, he strives for this flow to inform his own conduct. Eyes fixed straight ahead, he takes a clump of empty glasses in each hand and walks past, carefully, afraid to touch in case he breaks her spell.

Three feet of space behind the bar is not conducive to animated feats of flourish. Only when he approaches the glass-washer does he suddenly realize he can't put them down. With his fingers now impotent rolls of glassware, he can't remove one handful from the other. As he passes up behind her, she says,

"Calm down. They're just too stupid to understand that shouting and making a mess won't get them served any quicker. Take your time and do it properly."

58

Carrie has spoken. She frees his left hand for him, and he's given a fleeting grin. Immediately he wants to stop and reverse, check and make sure of it. He's sure he saw it...then it comes again.

"Besides, the less they drink, the less we have to stock up. Which means more for us."

Oh God. Through the fuzz of temporary idiocy, the words break through. Twice a plural pronoun, the 'we', the 'us', elevating him into her own orb, ramming into remission the leprosy that's been gnawing at his spine.

Evan forces a small smile, too afraid to speak in case this reprieve dissolves into another gaffe. If Carrie knew the effect she had on people, she'd be buckled with mirth and disbelief. Whilst on principle her quiet command of motion and speech would lend itself well to being a directress, a mistress, an assassin, a dictator, she'd never last in such consciously elevated positions of power. She'd be unable to take it even halfway seriously, mentally poking holes in arguments, wishing for solitude in which to do her own thing. Worlds may watch her, but Carrie won't watch back, eyes always focused on that space outside such stenciled shapes.

Then it's back to that swaddled couch, peeked at from corners of swaddled eyes. There's a frame frozen on the television screen, remote control abandoned on the coffee table. From the blur, Hilary can make out swatches of hot pink, undulations of corpulent flesh. It's the aria singer and the sobbing twins. The pair kneel before the great blob of flesh, its edges stretching the formation into a bottom-heavy triangle. The picture is too fuzzy to make out the faces, but there's something in the twins' angular prostration that hints at the likelihood of a tyrannical smirk on the chops of the chanteuse. Hilary sucks her teeth to keep her face together, and turns away from the screen. Lance twitches too much, he's being unprofessional and he knows it. They should have stopped at the bank, put in at least some effort to keep this simple, but once below deck the rules of commerce dissipate, rendering such efforts pointless. Cutting lines with business cards, snorting through the barrel of a Parker pen – it looks cool in the movies, but it cuts no ice with the real specialists. In Polly's office, the conventions undergo costume changes, and everything moves across the boards, riddled with trapdoors.

They wait for Polly's cue.

"How did you find the product?"

Lance and Hilary exchange glances. Be cool, don't rave, don't be a sucker.

"We're very interested in making an investment," Lance begins. "However, we're still unsure as to what that would entail."

"So...you're here to discuss a price."

"Yes. You see, we've been searching for something of superior quality, both reliable and affordable. From what we've gathered, you operate an individual apportioning of value, as opposed to a *prix fixe.*"

Polly stands, spreading her arms to match her smile. The fabrics flutter in wings, sweeping the breadth of the room, framing opulence for consumption.

"I believe very much that sensory pleasures should never be measured in monetary means. Like the theatre, like the arts, these privileges belong to everyone. In the same way, even the poorest of my clients has plenty to give in return. It just depends on how much they value what I provide...and what they are prepared to do for it."

At this, Polly points to the screen behind. Uncertainty prevails: this could be as sweet or as horrifying as dictated by a mood, by a trend, by the slightest variation in hue or tone. The celluloid captures only by contract, but the contents are to be determined by the whims of the director. Form and function have no meaning as yet, save from the vestiges of the yellow licking at the lips of the customers.

"We're...very, very keen to do business. If you would just explain..."

Hilary's speech is peppered by the eerie chattering of teeth. "I mean, you want to *film* us? Is that it? Doing what, exactly?"

"Oh, dear, it's so much more than mere *filming.* You are to be my works of art, my stars, welcome additions to my theatrical elite. There is no script and no audience save from your fellow players. I am not asking you to act, either – but to be acted upon. All you must do is take the stage and follow instructions."

Brows knit, knuckles creak, sweat beads all without prompting or prosthetics. Having laid out the payment, she reaches under the table for the casket of reward. Opening the lid, she presents the promise to the fidgeting prospectors. The packages inside are still mere cellophane and wrapper, but now, balmed in the awareness of their potency, they seem to exude a glow, a promise, to the susceptible magpies seated before them.

Plans are made. Without the aid of a schedule or script, these are but sketches, delineating an appointed time, an appointed evening – all that is certain is the raising of a curtain.

As planned, they arrive in plain clothing, an hour early. They are forbidden to exchange names or numbers with any other guests: such fraternization breaks the fourth wall of the stage, and deemed déclassé.

The show takes place on the third floor, directly below Polly's chamber, in a miniature version of the main auditorium. An echoing cavern painted dull red, high ceilings disappearing into the gloom. A rickety dais provides a pivot, around which three blocks of mismatched chairs revolve. These attest to the clandestine quality of the performance space – orange plastic seats from institutional waiting-rooms rub alongside low, chubby stools in primary colors, like those found in children's areas of cheap eateries. Some are musty red-velvet amputees torn from other music halls and abandoned playhouses, yearning for their glory days. There are no windows up here, therefore no need for blackout blinds. Still, heavy drapes depend from iron rods – more to mask hidden spectators than for the privacy of performers.

There is no stage door. Hilary and Lance wait in a cubby-hole of a dressing room along a short corridor, listening to feet shuffling past to fill the seats. Then comes a dusky thud of a heavy door, followed by the slamming of padlocks. This is the five-minute warning. There is no going back. Now, nobody may enter, and nobody may leave. A pitcher of Mojito cocktails, sticky with minted sugar, melts carelessly on the dressing table. It is unnecessary. Polly waits outside with a cough drop gleaming in each hand; lubricating the stars before they take to the stage. Lance and Hilary are already gone, beyond the need for Dutch courage or the appeal to break legs. The only propulsion required is the promise of another hit.

Full again with bursts of shimmering yellow, every movement in the sultry moisture of the dressing room is a performance of intrigue, a keen display of the feats trapped within their once-more flawless bodies. They're now more than ready – they're eager to get out there. To hide themselves would be most unfair. To keep the secrets of their physicality would be to sell themselves short, a thwarting of potential. They can't bury their charm, it must be shared and admired. Firmly stuck within the locked frame of their reflected brilliance, they risk blindness or immolation – they must disperse it into the waiting, wailing, drooling crowds. Everyone deserves a hit of wonder and sensory pleasure – taking the stage is the least they can do to further the ends of their slavering fellows.

Polly knocks at the door, then barges in without awaiting a reply. Over each arm she carries a black cowl of nankeen, in each palm rests a tiny berry of deepest red.

"Here. Take these, but first, put the hoods on. We always start the show in a costume of complete anonymity, to allow for the words to take spotlight."

Lance is appalled. Having spent so much time glistering at every available reflection, he's not ready to cloak his magnificence, to drown in it.

"You can't be serious. We can't wear those...nobody will be able to *see* us."

Polly nods. They still don't understand – it's for the best, for now. She is, however, used to managing the conduct of divas. She is a peerless ego masseuse – all she has to do is spin a few tall tales and rely on the reds to back it up.

"You'll appreciate the reasons behind it once you're out there. I can't have the audience *overwhelmed* by the pair of you right away – for the show to hold its grip, one must dispense the treats slowly, selectively. You don't want them to *gorge* on you, only to sicken with indulgence, do you?"

"Erm...I guess not..."

"The hoods will come off in the second act. We're going to show you off a little at a time, to hold the attention, to prolong the tantalization."

Hilary sees the point, almost. She's read enough in glossy magazines and made sufficient miscalculations on ill-advised dates to know that less is recommended as more. It wouldn't do to sleep with the audience and never have them call back.

"Sort of like a...striptease?"

Polly moves to clap her hands in glee, before remembering and stopping just in time to avoid crushing the pills.

"Exactly! You're a natural!"

It's not until the show begins that the real striptease begins.

Part VI

The debris was to be expected, in all fairness. Carrie can't be in two places at once, no matter how convincing the illusion perpetrated by her casual, yet effective, handling of the room and everything in it.

She and Lance lean on the bar as the door creaks closed on the final patron, and without cue, sigh the same breath of exhaustion. She can't help but be impressed. The stripling had made good in the end – taking it slowly, he'd begun to move with the rhythms of the pub. Cutting the angst from the proceedings saved time; time squandered worrying about mess, crumbling under demands, trying to produce something from nothing. She wonders how old he is, where he's from, what he's doing here. He's barely opened his mouth except to invite orders and mutter apologies.

"What are you having?" she asks. "The place is ours for now, and we're in charge of the comps book."

"Em…just a pint. Tennents, if that's okay."

She suppresses a howl of derision. He definitely needs to work on sucking freebies from the fruits of his labour. Tennents is anathema to the discerning drinker. Watery piss from the local brewery, still stinking of melted copper and stale hops. Cheap: tastes like it, too.

"I take it you're not much of a drinker."

This is another potential pitfall. To agree or disagree – both hold so many slings and arrows, each choice carrying an uncomplimentary label. To be a drinker in Glasgow was to be either a sot or a hard man. To be temperate was to be a wet blanket, or worse, a pussy. A gelatinous mass of fragility, lacking the prerequisite iron stomach that comes as standard in the Glaswegian physiognomy. He fears the implications of the latter too much to wish to avoid those of the former, answering,

"Oh, yeah, I like a drink as much as the next bloke. Why do you ask?"

"Tennents – a bit amateurish, wouldn't you say?"

He wouldn't know. He opts for the moral high ground.

"I guess so – it's just that it's cheap, and I don't want to take the piss when it's free."

Carrie shakes her head. She has to stick around now, just to give the poor guy an education. He'll learn.

"Look, you can have whatever you want. I don't know if you know, but I'm kind of an unofficial member of the management team here. I take what I want, and you're doing the same. Right?"

Evan breaks into a shy smile, an oddly compelling juxtaposition of confidence and sheepishness. He's not bothered about the drink – it's not that for which he's grateful. It's the generosity, the apparent interest the girl is taking in securing for him a offering of sufficient worth. The hint that, perhaps, he's worth something too.

"I guess so. What do you recommend?"

Mischief flares across Carrie's face, over her scalp, rippling her spinal cord.

"How's about some cocktails?"

This is her favorite means of pushing the parameters of luxury. She enjoys making them almost as much as she likes drinking them. Something about the crackle of liqueur over ice, the solid weight of the shaker in the hand, the dregs left at the bottom to chase with a straw.

"Sure, sounds good."

"Take a seat. I'll need a bit of space."

Evan moves around to the other side, and pulls a stool up to the counter to watch.

Musical chitterings, metal on metal, glass gliding on marble, working up to the crescendo of a symphony with no name. Promising thump of spirit bottles on aluminum. She works in silence, eyes narrowed in concentration, as the reeds of her fingers cage limes for slicing. Squeezed into the shaker with a wince, acid running into and over tiny cuts from the shift's minor casualties. Ice left until last, more room for spirits than mixer. Gin, vodka, grenadine, bitters, more: unknown substances in a cloudburst of colour and of variable viscosity. All running into spirit measures flickering between fingers like dancing batons, then crowned with a cursory scoop of ice for good measure. A bell rings out, welcoming a service, as the lid hits the shaker. Then the real performance begins. She looks away, into the depths of the room, grips the bottom of the shaker, and throws it into the air with a rattle of ice. It hangs for what seems like forever, spinning wildly, throwing shafts of white light in a spiraling cloud, before pirouetting back down into Carrie's waiting hand. All without a glance, a twitch, a fidget: all movement restricted to a flick of the wrist.

She stands with her prize for a moment or two, a bullfighter fluttering her flag before a bow. Meeting Evan's eyes, which bulge, stunned, from the sockets, she breaks her hold and grins, slamming the shaker onto the bar with a resounding thud.

"Wow...where'd you learn how to do that?"

Carrie shakes her head, casting off the masquerade. She's a talker or a mover, but rarely both at once. She lacks the necessary conceit to wax lyrical about her acts of fancy. Besides, she's not finished yet. Removing the cap from the shaker, she decants the contents into two waiting Martini glasses, still frosted from the chill cabinet. It's a bizarre color, pushing out different tones of purple, green, blue, red like pure light diffracted through a lens.

"Cherry or olive?

She's a cherry fan herself, but keenly aware that her sweet tooth isn't a common trait among all and every tippler. She skewers six of them along a cocktail stick, resting it on the ledge of her own glass.

Evan's now so spellbound he's unable to make decisions for himself. He plays it safe, averting his eyes as she drains the lees from the shaker with a plastic straw.

"I'll have what you're having."

She finishes his with the same garnish, then attaches cocktail straws to the side of the glasses. She holds back from whacking in miniature umbrellas. This was the proper, dignified article, not a beachwear accessory.

Carrie leaves the bar, pulls up next to Evan, and they contemplate the objets d'art, almost too beautiful to drink.

"Cheers."

They each take a delicate sip, leaning over the glasses instead of moving them. A concoction of almost pure alcohol, it has little to sweeten but the cherry syrup, yet coats the mouth in a blissful enamel, liquid opal. To be sipped slowly, savoured, drawn out in anticipation of the next one.

"So...that was pretty cool."

Evan wants to wrench his tongue out, so irked is he by this seemingly endless supply of pointless conversational dead-ends. It's a fucking minefield – he wants to ask so many questions, but he's afraid of fouling the air with inanity. He tries once more.

"I mean, are you a professional cocktail-maker?"

Christ. That's probably the wrong terminology. He waits. Her lips are still poised over the glass. Arcing her neck back in the wake of the taste, she rolls it around her mouth before answering.

"No. I just picked it up, coming here all the time when I was a kid. My dad used to work on the bar, and I'd watch him do tricks with the bottles and glasses. On quiet days, when there were no customers around, he'd take me behind the bar and show me how. Just a daft thing...nothing special."

This is the most she's uttered in a single stream over the duration of the evening, exhaled in a volley of near-sighs. She looks straight ahead as she speaks, caught in a reverie. Her eyes play among the shimmering bottles, lit up from behind, throwing harlequin shapes across the contours of her complexion. A lower lip curls up into the clutch of her upper incisors, her brows narrow, closing the curtains on her face.

"I've never seen anything like that before. Your dad must have been *something*."

Evan has to take care here, decidedly delicate. He can tell from the whispering, from the stopping-up of mouth and eyes, that this may be a secret history of sorts. He knows, even through his tendency to awkwardness, that there's more to come, or more to hide. The father is etched into past tense. He must be gone, like his own.

"Yeah. He was. Glad he left me something useful...although my mother would beg to differ. You've got be on top of things nowadays, particularly in a seller's market like a bar. Softens the financial blow when you get a show with your drink, I've noticed."

For an artist, she'd adept at rendering such endeavors to points of business. A thick wedge of cynicism opens up in her address, something Evan's encountered often in his dialogues with fellow students. Broken idealists seem to congregate in palaces of learning or drinking dens. Everyone who still cared enough seemed to be seeking a tonic of some kind to assuage the blank chill of the recession.

But she's talking to him.

Carrie isn't sure why he's still here, why he's watching her like that. She can tell, from the fuzzed outline in her peripheral vision, that he's actually interested in listening. His head cocked aslant on the

66

gangling neck. The tip of the thumb rubbing at the underside of the glass. The slow nod.

"I don't come out to the city very often," he begins, "But I've noticed, when I do, how impatient people have become. It's like they don't want to look away from some...fixed target hanging there somewhere. 'Get out of my way, don't dare talk to me' – that kind of thing."

"Or they're afraid of catching sight of themselves in the faces of other people."

Carrie turns and faces him properly, for the first time. He feels the weight of her gaze moving across each muscle contraction, each impact of lip on lip, tongue on teeth. He turns to the cocktail and relies upon the known action to carry the load of her stare for a borrowed second, before replying.

"I know what you mean. The more difficult it is to get folks' attention, the less open they are to having it piqued in the first place. That's why what you do is so cool: it's the kind of thing that shuts people up, makes them watch and listen. I know I couldn't let that go by without comment, without breaking stride to have a proper look."

She smiles. This is unexpected...she has no repertoire of circus feats or magic tricks. All she does, really, is move things around in an interesting way, throwing objects into the air and hoping that they'll land where she'd planned. Flairing is the mathematics to her artistic predilections, something to keep both sides of the brain ticking over. Chasing paint around a canvas is her lifeblood, but sometimes she needs an outcome whereby the success of the venture is clearly marked. In the bar, it's obvious – spilt drinks, broken glasses, and the laughing maw of the slobbering spectators.

"It's dead easy. A bit of geometry, a healthy respect for physics, and the ability to act like you don't care if it all goes tits-up."

Self-deprecation is a trait Evan recognizes in others with a keenness much more honed than he does in himself. He takes pains to address it without wishing to plumb depths of obsequy. He doesn't know, yet, that the apparent irreverence granted to the skill is as a direct consequence of Carrie's disappointment with her teacher. The ability to flair is all that's left of him in her, and it grates to bear something so fleeting.

"If that's the case, you manage extremely well. I certainly couldn't do it."

"Stick around here for long enough, and I'll show you. It's certainly easier to get a grip on than some of the freaky stuff that goes on in the rest of this place."

He has to, now. Every distillation of though and motion is there before him, might be there for as long as he can hold down the job.

"I think I will. I like this place. You're right, it is a bit mad, but that's half of the appeal."

He need not strangle his slowly-building credibility by adding that the other half sits beside him in a faultless composition: legs scissored, arms unfurling like pennants, hands and lips framing the liquor, tinting her face with a pentane rainbow.

"Then that's half the battle, too," Carrie breathes. "Too many people walk in here, get a glimpse of the insanity, and walk right back out again. Polly does that to folk: plays around in their extremities, pushes their limits. Not always in a cool, edgy, underground-culture kind of way, either. Sometimes she's just a fucking nutcase, and that's all there is to it."

Part VII

The reds have dropped. The show is in swing.

Bright lights. They all fall down, into the trampettes waiting to catch and re-launch each soaring ego. Neither questions nor comments have marks or stains. Instead, truth rumbles like a snare drum in an empty canyon, bouncing forth and back, forth and back, twirling batons aflame at either end.

Ruddy faces, shining with peanut oil and popcorn butter, leer from, the pit. They drool into laps, delighting in Hilary's refusal to colour with shame. This has to be the punch line. It has to be.

Polly strides onstage, in a chain-mail tabard no less alarming for its plasticity. Spanning more than one era, more than two halves, on her bouffant she sports a miniature top hat. Into the hatband are fixed two long, silver cigarette holders, freshly-lit tapers glowing at the tips.

She passes one to Hilary.

"Stand up."

She rises from the chair on quaking knees. Polly frees Lance's arms from behind the post, and presents him with the other flammable. Then she addresses the audience.

"Here, human detritus: as fit for ashtrays as for shallow fucks and cheap deals. Don't you think?"

The sweating, howling spectators cheer, thumping the floor with heels, umbrellas, silver-topped walking sticks.

"They chose their crimes. They shall choose the criminal."

Polly drags Hilary by the wrist across the stage, to stand beside her co-star. She slaps her, hard, across her bare shoulders. Lance receives a no less perfunctory blow to the jaw. Still anaesthetized with red, he doesn't flinch.

"Which of you is most terrible? Who requires punishment? It's one or both. Act or act upon. Extinguish the flame on whichever of you has incurred the greatest penalty."

She turns again to the audience.

"It's him or her. But not neither. Whatever happens, both will pay up."

Polly executes a lesson in philosophy. Her customers, her audience, all who populate her world, come down to this. They become what they repeatedly do. Tonight's lesson is brief, for a matinee audience with an abbreviated attention span. Hilary and Lance behave like animals. Like animals, they will be branded as such.

Grinding, chewing, never ceasing, the red's the thing. They will now do anything, say anything, be anything to anyone, caged in the frames of a million webbed hand and fingers. It's difficult to fathom at first why the rest of them look so fucking *happy* – as though amid this chaos, this ceremony of degradation, this ghoulish Mardi Gras, their lives as glistening pearls, fermentations beyond their wildest dreams. It's a crock. It's a machination. They smile and cheer, sweat and grovel, because Polly wills it so. It's second-hand ether, used breath, twice-oxygenated and spat back out, uselessness.

Conversations long since stultified, pickled in piss and vinegar, leached and sucked dry and pieced together from crossword-puzzle clues. But still it works. They feel nothing.

Everything up until now has been a long line at a ticket booth, waiting, rubbing hands together in preparation for the purchase of another colossal disappointment. The ticket-master punches the holes with his teeth, printing the price tag with his finely honed grin. He accepts no callbacks, awards no refunds nor cancellations, each purchase final with statutory rights affected without remorse.

This; this is something else. Something unprecedented, without equal. This defies the power of sloganeering. It needs no advertisement; once tried and tested, the loyal consumers strung up by the books. This is the red. This is suspended animation, cessation of any further pondering. No questions are asked where none can be answered. This is the holding pattern, right there in the spectacle, untouched and immovable. This cannot be captured in glossy print nor column inches, the horrible luminescence, the stunning obscenity. Stars pour down throats and solidify, weighing down the recipients with the weight of the watching universe.

The guy in the back has nothing left to lose. He raises his hands and cries,

"I'll do it, I'll do it again. Let me speak."

Polly, a center-stage totem, flings her wingspan open once more, and beckons with the tips of her fingers.

"Please, do come on up. There's plenty for everybody."

The man swings from side to side as he barrels up the aisle, checking, perhaps, for faces he knows. He runs the last three yards, then thumps onto the stage on both feet, grabbing the microphone stand in front of Polly.

"NO!" Polly yells, wresting it back. "SIT DOWN!"

She pushes him into the chair, and grabs him by the head with spread fingers.

"The same rules apply. You sit, you wait, you do what you're told, and you speak only when you're spoken to. Understood?"

The man nods, looking not at the audience but into the distance, at the reward staining the fabric of everything within his skull. Polly reaches behind the seat and produces a pair of leather arm-buckles, into which she clamps the newcomer's wrists.

The trio take the stage, lining up behind the seated player. The one on the middle, the tallest, fits a mask over the face of the man. White plastic, blank cherubic, slits for eyes and a hole drilled between the pursed lips.

"Now, you're in the elite because you have a secret. You're flawed. We seek to repair you through this channel, dispersing your transgressions into the audience. By the medium of artistic address, we can bring you back to your true self. We reverse pretence. We abhor lies. Speak, and tell the rest why you are here."

A pause. The man, still cockily drumming his fingers on his knees, apparently unruffled by his bondage, begins. His voice rings out in a booming echo, oratory skills perfected in boardrooms and torture chambers.

"I was born down by the docks a time ago. My old man was a welder, my mam was a nurse. I had six brothers and two sisters, all of us crammed into this wee tenement flat. We were poor. I never had anything I wanted, anything my pals had. I always knew I was fit for something better. So I went for it. Started talking to the right people, beating up the bams who gave me shite…"

Polly is not impressed. She gives a nod to the trio. The middle player grabs the man by the hair, wrenching him back, tilting the chair. The other two provide a box to each ear. The bellow of pain echoing inside the mask is horrendous, death under the sea, in a hollow tube.

"What makes you think you can do better than the last act? You must have a real story to tell, a reason. Why else would we be listening to you, still? Get on with it."

"I'm the richest man ever made good from the back end of the Barrowlands. Just the gift of the gab, y'see, I coulda selt sand tae the blacks. By the time I wis twenty-two, I had a house in every major city in the world. I had a sports car for every day of the week. I had a wife – model, fuckin' gorgeous. All I had to do was send a few packages here and there, pick up a few payments. I had everything, but I was never satisfied. I always wanted more. I wanted bigger fish. So I shipped out to Italy. The wife didn't like it there, said it was too hot. I told her to fuck off back home if she didn't like it, and before she's even stepped on a plane I had a new bird. I was a respectable fella. Never smoked a day in my puff, never drank, never hit the wife for no good reason.

"Then the traffic started. Some fella gave me twenty grand to drive a truck from one end of the country to another. Couple of tons of gear inside, but at twenty grand for a day's work I wasnae gonnae argue. Then I started taking a wee bit here and there. Got tae the point I was sticking half the market value of my villa up my snout every week. But I couldnae stop. It was too fuckin' good, I was a mess without it.

But don't get me wrang. I never got busted, never got into debt. Nothing bad ever happened, except that thing with the deid wummin. I'm no a bad guy, it wisnae me that kilt her. But it wis enough to get me thinking about going straight. That night, I took a gram that blew my mind. My eyeballs had fuckin' feet, crawling doon oot ma face. I decided tae can the Charlie. After a few false starts, I did it. I'm a decent fuckin' citizen noo."

A crack, a snap, the sound of a firmament rendered to pieces. Darkness falls over the theatre; proper darkness. No seep of sodium from outside streetlamps, no glow from mobile phones, no red pinpricks. Polly rings out from the voice, solidifying the mass of pitch, setting the every limb and nerve to stone.

"Merchant! You lie."

Her voice is aural poison, verdigris running from the microphone stand, down the wires, coating the room in a cavernous echo. Spotlights illuminate the speaker's head and torso, Polly's feet, masking her face.

"Tell the truth, merchant. The woman."

Silence, save from a humming refutation from beneath the cherub mask. He won't talk, he can't go back there. Polly knows this. The mimes have left the stage in the absence of light, and in their place come the twins. Each followed by their own fox-fire, saucer-sized glimmers playing over the bodies, away from the face. Their lithe bodies give them away, their pink Mohawks, if present, are out of sight.

They're dressed in flower-sprigged nightgowns, swinging from shoulders to ankles, swirling them along the dais in a foam of white lace. The speaker groans, terrified, as they dance around and around the seat, circling him like prey. Polly watches as the twins lean into the man, twisting their bodies against and around the player who refuses to play. No music, no sound; save for the whisper of dry cotton on naked skin, the pattering of bare feet, the low moan from the depths of the mask, slowly increasing in pitch.

"RIGHT, I'LL TELL! I'LL TELL!"

"Fabulous. Enough, girls."

They move to the rear of the stage and stand, still obscured from the neck up.

"I was doing a deal with a fella whose wife was a bit…funny in the head, y'know. Lovely lassie, but a few screws loose. Her fella fucked me over for a kilo, and I don't take that lightly. I had to pay him a wee visit. Not to hurt him, you see…just to have a bit of a chat. I'm no a violent man!"

He breaks off at this last, his voice gliding to a shriek, a plea.

"Go on. What happened on this *visit* of yours?"

"Me and the gaffer got there to a locked door. Pair of great big fuckin' Rottweilers outside, gasping and panting like nothing else in that heat. Their water-bowls were empty. They looked all…sucked dry, like they'd been there for a while. We knocked and knocked, and there wis no answer. Gaffer's a bit nervous, like. Says the fella's been threatening to dae his wife in, she's been threatening to take the money and run for it. So what we're looking at here is nae gear, nae money, nae negotiation, unless we can get intae the hoose. You huv tae understand – this was big-league stuff. We couldnae play silly buggers.

So we broke in. Took a tire iron tae the patio door. Had a wee rummage, and took the gear."

Again he halts, hoping for a reprieve, hoping this is enough.

"That's not all though, is it?"

"We stopped for a test run. Chopped out a few lines on the kitchen table. Then we remembered the fella and his wife. See, when we tried to break in at first, with a jimmy, it wouldnae work because there was a key in the lock. The door was locked from the inside. There had to be somebody in the house."

"You didn't check before you sat down for a line?" Polly asks, sweetly, as though talking through a problem-solving exercise with an imbecile.

"Naw. You don't, do you? When it's there, it's in your hand, and you've been wrestling with a fuckin' door for half an hour…it takes over."

"Was it…good? Was it of sufficient quality?" Polly presses on, still honeyed.

"It was…fuckin' brilliant. Never had anything like it. Sitting at that kitchen table, sunlight comin' through the blinds…felt like I'd arrived, ye know?"

"Then what happened?"

If it were visible, the face below the mask would be a crumpled wreck. The man can't speak for a moment or two, choking on the words as he unravels the reality from the high.

"Then the gaffer and me remember about the lock. That there must be somebody in the house. So we have to go looking. He started downstairs, I went to the check the upstairs bedrooms. The first one was empty. But the second…I couldn't get in at first. There was something blocking the door. So I pushed and pushed, you know - with that *coke* strength you get. It finally swung open. At first I couldnae figure out what was blocking it – there was nothing there. Then it swung shut, and…there she was. Hangin' aff the back of the door."

There is a pause, a silence in which every heartbeat in the room is audible. The spotlights on the twins are almost imperceptibly expanding. Something along the neckline of the nightgown begins to move, to slink from around the shoulders.

"Man, she was fuckin' stinkin', must have been there for days. Hangin' there in her nightie. Pished herself too, as ye do when yer deid. And I'm telling ye, she was blacker in the face than she was white in the arms and legs."

74

The player begins to shake, the chair shaking with him as he struggles with his bonds.

"We couldnae do anything! We had a fuckin' nosebag in the glove compartment and a gun in the boot. Couldnae phone the polis. By then we'd touched everything in the house, our prints were all over. We had tae leave, or they'd have though it wis us who'd done her in."

Hisses of disgust issue from the audience. Polly isn't ready yet for a finale, and coaxes, soothing, gentle.

"Of course...of course. You took what you'd come for, and left, didn't you? You left that woman hanging on the back of the door, and made for the road. Didn't your conscience bother you?"

"Naw, she wis deid, nothing we could dae. But that face stuck around for a long time - especially when I was buzzing. Took the pleasure out of the gear, for me, anyway. I never spoke to her fella again. Left the country and got my act together. See what I mean? I'm no a bad guy."

The twins move forward from the rear of the stage, to stand behind the man. His mask is removed, hung over the back of the seat. Each twin unbuckles a strap, freeing the prisoner's arms. He rolls his wrists around in relief. All the while the spotlights are growing wider, brighter.

"Well done. Excellent performance. You're free to go," says Polly, "But one last thing, merchant. Give your regards to your last customer."

The twins are lit up, surrounding the player on both sides. Stuffed, shining, swollen gourds loll freakishly from their slender necks. Faces purpled and distended, bursting out over the top of a ring of patent belts. Their eyes extend further and wider than human physiology permits, the bottom edges touching the cheekbones. The tongues protrude like extra limbs, black and yellow and oozing with the excretions of a protracted death. They reach to the merchant, straining fingers, flicking wrists.

He screams, tries to stand, to run, trips over the chair. Still they extend their ghastly embrace, looming over his trembling form.

Polly raises a hand. The lights go out once more. The room plunges into near nothingness, held in the realm of the physical only by a strangled, dwindling scream.

Part VIII

After the private shows, Polly winds down in her own suite. She has every confidence in her personnel. They will oversee the discussions, neutralize any hostilities, dispense the refreshments and unlock the doors when the time is right.

A dry flutter of wings from the bird cage. They're awake, still, waiting a feed. She opens a carton of chocolates, picks out the ones containing nuts, and crumbles them through the bars. The lovebirds whistle their appreciation. Polly bows; twirling hand over hand, then sits down with her remote control and the rest of the confectionary. A prepared tray rests on the coffee table, encompassing a decanter of brandy, a soda siphon, a pewter bucket of ice and a matching egg-cup of cellophaned delicacies. Yellow tonight. It's been a tiring evening, and she wishes a leisurely slide into sopoforia.

From the corner, a shifting, the slink of nylon on hessian. Mike groans around the rubber gag. She should really take him for a stretch, but it's late and she can't quite summon the energy. He'll have to wait until morning. She stands, ambles over to the sideboard and picks up a highball glass, a metal straw. Into this she sloshes a generous amount of brandy, before crouching next to the bound bartender. Inserting the end of the straw into the corner of his mouth, slipping it past the muzzle, she pats him on the head and sighs softly through the nose.

"Drink this down, sweetheart. It will help you sleep."

Mike slurps, his eyes rolling back in the lesser of two evils. He calms, stops moaning, and tilts his head back to lean against the wall.

"The show went very well tonight, you'll be pleased to hear. Possibly among the best of the run so far."

Mike snorts as best he can through the obstructions. He doesn't give a shit about her fucking shows. All he wants to know is whether

Carrie is alright: information with which Polly is unable to furnish him, having neither knowledge nor interest herself.

The final rumble from the bottom of the glass signals the end of Mike's repast. He glares at Polly, jerks his head back to remove the straw, and turns away. He nestles his chin into the crook of his neck and waits for the air to leave the room.

Carrie is more than fine. She's at that elusive stage of inebriety at which everything glistens and wavers; just slightly enough to take the edge off of reality. Resentment at having to be sociable has been overthrown by a pleasant appreciation of the present company.

Trying to pinpoint what it is about him that makes him tolerable occupies her thoughts for a slow sip. It strikes her that perhaps it's the rare quality of kindness lacking entirely in interference. He offers neither advice nor bubble-wrapped criticism – purely an exchange of words and ideas, dialogue between equals.

She deliberately avoids opening the casket of melancholy that attends most discussions of absent parents. It's enough, for now, to be united in their sway under a clanking matriarchy. His mum sounds nice, nicer than her own, but much too involved. He gets this hangdog expression when he mentions her: being both grateful for her attentions, yet aware of his intermittent spurts of ingratitude when it comes to her over-involvement in his affairs. All too aware of its killjoy capabilities, he limits talk of his mother to the incidental and peripheral.

Carrie finds herself much more interested in hearing about his university career. She has unlimited unconditional offers from a host of the most established institutes of higher education, and is keen to hear what she's in for when she finally breaks from the hedgerow-choked constraints of suburbia.

"Is it like the movies, then? Loads of intellectuals, walking deftly around, looking super-cool in their respective microcosms of individuality? Partying until the wee hours and coming to lectures still pissed, smoking clove cigarettes?"

Evan chuckles; enjoying this opportunity to be the one with the insider's knowledge. He wishes he had more to tell. Living at home instead of in student residences means he misses out on a considerably large portion of student life. A few fly pints in the union between lectures doesn't quite match up to the forty-eight hour benders legendary among certain of his classmates.

"Bits and pieces...certainly a lot of drinking, a lot of weird clothing, and a *hell* of a lot of pretentious pseudo-philosophers wandering around in berets and winkle-pickers."

Evan gets the impression that loads of the people get their ideas of what students wear, how they act, from watching movies themselves. The resultant effect is one of fluid, amorphous, possibly inbred movements of style and substance, each constantly upstaging the other, impossible to track for longer than a semester at a time. Evan doesn't bother trying. He can't tell Carrie for fear of shattering any illusions – he has no doubt she'd rule the campus if she set her mind to it – but he's pretty lonely. University isn't what he'd imagined, and he finds himself wandering into and out of the lectures and classes in a throng of faces he can't put names to, most of them laughing and joking with a bevy of cohorts. He's too shy to ask to tag along to any of their liquid lunches. Instead, he takes a book or a newspaper to the union. There, he braves the humiliating ten-minute interval between paying for his lunch and finding a seat. – wandering the cafeteria through the walls of heavy laughter, tray in hand with its unspecified contents rapidly cooling and congealing, before finding a quiet niche in which to look busy and unruffled by his solitude.

"So you're not one of *them*, then? I can understand why – it takes too much effort to constantly fret about slotting perfectly into some sort of niche. Or even worse, working so hard on being *different* that you end up being exactly the same."

Carrie hasn't left this pitfall too far behind. At school, there's nothing between extremes in terms of garnering status in one subset or another. Prefixing any of the labels – trendy, hippy, Goth, geek, gangster – is the unspoken catechism '*the right kind of*'. Acceptance comes only with the right credentials, which are unattainable without sacrificing any remaining traces of energy, pleasure, individuality and sanity.

"Don't get me wrong. It'd be pretty cool to have that kind of conviction in my utter, unrivalled coolness. Those guys don't look like they give a fuck – like they were *born* to be big men on campus. They certainly don't lack followers....male and female," he replies, talking up the university poster boys, for the appearance's sake, if not his own. "...but I guess it takes time to be that self-assured. I'm only in my second year. I'm still getting my head around figuring out how much work – or how little – I need to do, to pass exams and stuff. The image thing's a work in progress."

Carrie looks thoughtful, chewing on her straw. The bowl of maraschino cherries sat on the bar between them has slowly depleted throughout their conversation, and the plastic seems to fill a gap in some hand-to-mouth action. She misses being able to smoke inside, even though she's too young to have been around for much of its heyday.

"I don't know. I guess I kind of thought that everything just...fell into place at uni. With your clothes, your mates, your music, your passions all *validated* somehow."

"Guess it's like anything else. It takes time."

This is Evan's stock solution to all problems, bequeathed by his mother. He's lost most of his faith in its efficacy – it's merely a thought-terminating cliché, encouraging the receiver to lay the matter at hand aside. On closer inspection, it means nothing at all. Time doesn't make much of a difference save for its softening effect on miseries and disappointments long past. In this case, he suspects that waiting around for things to change is about as effective as waiting for an equally cliché-swaddled miracle, seraphic choirs and tickertape announcing the naissance of a new and improved version of himself. He doesn't want to tell Carrie it's more likely that such things are just a letdown, the scale of which is usually proportionate to the hope invested in the sham. The promise of a call, with the fluttering of fingers, the air kisses. Waking up in arms unrecognizable from those into which you retired the previous evening. The smiling faces of the salespersons of whose clientele you are by far the best and brightest. The aperture between saying what is meant, and meaning what is said. The thundering chasm between actions and words, between lies and withholding the truth. He's only just at the very edge of having any kind of grasp himself.

He's still immersed in the task of gathering little nuggets of wisdom and truth. They remain stored in jars behind shop counters, dispensed in pence to pound by sneering shopkeepers, their grubby pinafores and lined hands holding no clues as to the provenance or utility of the product. Hopes remain scrunched into paper bags, as valuable used as thrown away. Time does not help, it merely watches, marking its own passage in palatable portions.

Now that it's half-empty, easier to manipulate without spillage, Evan draws his glass across the bar for another sip. He's remarkably sober, possibly as a consequence of the exercise of drinking running concurrent to actual thought and conversation, as opposed to a means of drowning drivel. He glances to the side, where Carrie has moved on from the straw and settled upon tinkling her fingernails on the bar taps. He remembers the gesture from the previous evening. Marking a territory, or intimating a desire.

"Carrie?"

The syllables taste strange, like the unexpected sweetness bursting from around the tight skin of a grape. A sound so much more satisfying than the spillage over the course of the evening: instead of the pointless cliff-edge struggles for the correct combination, this one arrives fully-formed, a perfect kernel in itself, yet left open-ended by its articulation, consonants pushing vowels out, ringing, into the light.

"Yeah? Sorry...I was in my own wee world, there. Thinking about time," she points to the brass and mahogany clock hanging before them, "and whether there's enough of it for one more. If you're up for it."

There is, of course, there always is. Strange, though – she's never hung behind with a perfect stranger. He's easy company. Seems to be holding his liquor as competently as she can. He'll make a bartender yet, perhaps a friend. So long as she keeps her trap closed on her less savory pet subjects.

Evan raises his eyebrows. It's nearly two o'clock. He's surprised, partially because he hasn't noticed the hours passing, and partially because her remark applies to them both. Fuck the morning lecture – if she wants him to stick around, he's not budging. He's suddenly aware of the missed opportunities possibly found alongside the less favorable consequences of taking risks. He spends too long deliberating. Now's the time to face the potential regrets of chances taken, as opposed to regrets of never having taken chances at all.

"I'm game if you are."

"Excellent. Why don't you take a shot – pardon the pun – and we'll see if you've picked anything up? Don't worry about the fancy shit. I think we can settle for lightly shaken, as opposed to any stunt maneuvers. Even I wouldn't the now, not after I've had a couple."

Evan surprises himself. It's so easy, here, without the walls of solid noise, the flailing hands. The same actions, the same motions, but with the removal of the squalls, the burning tapers flaring on the walls, the chaos, the task acquires a fluidity. He sees now why Carrie seems to enjoy it so much. The ritual creates a blurred frame, inside which the rest of the evening moves around.

He discovers he's making a palette to match her portrait, recreating her nuances as best he can in the limited scope of the shaker. Thick, dark Kahlua for her hair. Crisp, clean vodka in tribute to her voice and speech. Sharp flashes of Chambord for her lips, just enough for a tinge, a whisper, floating germs of truth far outweighing their twin ambassadors. Glugs of amber Amaretto fall far short of capturing her eyes. The flavor of sugared almonds over the warmth of the alcohol makes up slightly for the shortfall, almost like drinking the depths of the orbs themselves.

Those orbs are currently watching him. He's never held a gaze before. He's never been the focus of attention from such an unexpected source. He stands at the wide end of an hourglass, the base to which the concentration of sand crystals flow.

Keen to keep the colour as pure and true as possible, he shakes up the resultant mix with very little ice, relying on the chill from the frosted glasses to regulate the temperature. Fishing around in a miniature fridge below the bar, he unearths a fresh tub of cherries. Out of Carrie's line of sight, he follows her example from earlier, creating tiny totem poles from the fruit and some cocktail sticks. With a flourish, he stand upright and floats them atop the drinks, and grins with a pride utterly disproportionate to the accomplishment. He's rewarded with a beam from his companion, beautiful in spite of the slight embarrassment at his recognition of her sweet tooth.

"Well, I gave it my best. I can't promise anything, but at least there's plenty of alcohol in it."

"No, it looks brilliant. How did you know I liked Amaretto?"

"I took a guess. It's nice and…well, sweet, and I got the impression you were keen."

Carrie giggles, then silently admonishes herself for being so fucking *cute*. It doesn't sit well with the rest of her character. It's too much of a trite incompatibility, like a whore with a heart of gold, a gangster clutching a pet Chihuahua.

After first swirling a sip around her mouth, spreading the fluid across every inch of sensory surface area, she swallows, pursing her lips in thought.

"This is delicious. Thank you."

Evan closes his eyes in relief.

"No problem."

He starts on his own, waiting. Carrie stares at the far corner of the bar, still lost in rumination. Time for an anecdote. Something to put him in his place.

"Y'know, I *do* like sugary things, but it didn't start out that way because of the taste."

She flares her brows, a warning signal, runs the tip of her tongue across her teeth.

"Oh...? Sorry...I didn't mean..." Evan's confused, now, and worried he's misread her.

He's afraid he's taken liberties with his observations, that he's somehow breached a barrier into which she's unwilling to admit visitors. Carrie jumps in with a harsh laugh.

"I was being obstinate, as usual. I had to wear braces for years, even though I didn't think I needed them. They gave me this big packet of pamphlets and a long lecture on what I could and couldn't do. The orthodontist told me to stay away from sugary things, gum and toffee and fudge and lollipops, all sorts of stuff I wasn't ready to give up yet. I was mad as hell enough with a mouthful of metal – I kind of told him to go fuck himself, and proceeded to munch on anything I could get my hands on that was supposed to be bad for my teeth."

This is Carrie's raison d'etre. The breaking of rules, the disregard of sound advice.

"Didn't you get into trouble?"

"Every time. But, see, there wasn't a damn thing he could do about it. I didn't get any damage done. I brushed my teeth constantly, chewed carefully, even used the daft wee toothpick thingies they give you. I just wanted to prove to the smug bastard that he didn't know everything. That we've survived without orthodontists since we crawled out of the primordial stew, and that just because he's got a stupid white coat and an ear-bleeding salary doesn't make him indispensable."

As she talks, she tilts her head back, staring straight ahead. She's jutting out a chin at an invisible monster, full even now of the conviction of everything she does.

"I did it, too. Never had a filling, never broke my braces, didn't fuck up my teeth while they were on. I'll never forget his face when he took them out and there was nothing to see but enamel. No food for the soul quite like getting one over on someone who thinks they're always right."

Carrie feels no need to mention that the man in question was an authority figure on the brink of ridicule in more ways than one. He'd been fucking her mother. He had tried to fuck her, too, one drunken evening. That was enough, as past experience had taught her, to nullify any granules of truth in anything he cared to impart. It took tremendous self-control not to bite his fingers off the next time they found her mouth. If he'd tried once more out of the context of the dentist's chair, he may not have been so lucky.

Evan doesn't need to hear this. She doesn't want to tick another box to fit a two-dimensional prototype. She'd only reel off a string of jokes, or self-deprecate to the point at which he'd feel the need to step in and redress the balance. Truth need not be a case of full disclosure, a cross-section, the flapping reels of newsprint rolling off the presses. If she's learned anything from drifting around the theatre all this time, it's how to drop layers of self in wafer-thin slices, curling around the feet in scarves of many colors.

Part XI

The minivan outside is bright red, lurid even under cover of darkness. Nothing in the city can move in spectrum silence for long. It look like a shrunken London tour-bus, an effect augmented by the driver standing to attention at the passenger door. All in black, with a peaked cap, his posture supplies the authority, his full-face mask supplies the anonymity. He holds in one hand a silver box with a slit at the top, presumably for tips. The other hand is clutched into a fist at the end of a rigid arm, pressed tightly to his side.

The twins are no longer dead. They wear simple white suits; pencil skirts and blazer jackets, piped around the edges and sleeves with scarlet satin. Having their makeup removed has somehow wiped away all other defining characteristics – if Hilary had been fit to scrutinize her escorts, she would struggle to make out an eye colour, a quirk in profile, a skin tone. Thus they move with the bands of red around their attire, like chalk marks on a crime scene brought to life.

They take the front of the procession of spectators. They halt at the door, speechlessly inciting the followers to do the same. Coming up at the rear of the stupefied crocodile is the opera singer. Instead of her lurid bikini, she wears a thickly starched linen tunic in khaki green, her wild hair slicked back into a tight roll. Like the twins, her face is bare, save for chiseled notches running from each nostril to the corners of her mouth and down her chin, like a rubber-bandaged mannequin.

She's had an easy time of it tonight. There's been no need for intercession onstage. Still, Polly knows only too well that sometimes accidents happen, and there's no harm in having some visibly robust authority present in case of emergency. The chanteuse speaks to the backs of the congregants' heads, her voice booming through the lobby, causing the chandeliers to tinkle. It's rougher than Lance remembers from the performance of the previous evening. It's no longer necessary to entertain, nor enthrall. It's time for orders.

"Take a token each. Give it to the driver. He will take you directly home. No unscheduled stops, no diversions, no disruptions to the itinerary, no questions, no comments. Understood?"

Mutely, the travelers agree. There will be no trouble tonight.

The twins lead the first eight members out to the minivan, leaving the rest in the charge of the opera singer. Some have to be folded into the vehicle, motor control left behind in the theatre. Once the doors slam closed on the passengers, the driver salutes the twins, marches to the front of the van and takes possession of the wheel.

The van is silent as it pulls away. Polly's flair for illusion clearly extends even to manipulating mechanics.

Hilary and Lance are in the second batch, to wait in the lobby whilst the first group is dispatched. Probably more local, a sharper drop-off. Swifter disposal of evidence.

The silence in the lobby takes on a corporeal form, pressing down upon the waiting crowd, asphyxiating them all beneath the weight of the unspoken.

Moving in perfect synchrony, the twins ascend the steps once more, before bracing the room between their outspread arms. Then they speak, in one voice. With no variations in tone, mono produced from stereo, the sound swallows all, the unitarian oration of a higher power.

"You may speak among yourselves. Just remember; anything you say now belongs to us. Choose your words wisely."

Of course, nobody says a word, at first. No players dare look at any of the others, the full impact of the preceding spectacle writ large on their stricken faces.

Eventually the brush of Lance's sleeve against her bare arm becomes too much for Hilary. Tingling, every hair shoved sickeningly erect, both she and her brother are too hopelessly present to deny.

"Look, will you just calm it? Stop your fucking twitching, you're giving me hives."

Lance says nothing. Calmly, slowly, he folds his arms, clamping them into his sides. His jaws work overtime. He says more with their crunching, scraping of teeth over teeth, than he could in words. He takes a step to the side, his quivers more noticeable now without Hilary to bolster his shakes. Words and phrases rattle around inside, loose teeth in a long-buried skull. He can't trust enough in his powers of speech to bring them to light.

It appears there's a flaw in Polly's argument for sensation. Once all the partitions are breached, after all the buildings have fallen down into their own foundations, there's nothing left to reach for. Nothing can surpass the fulfillment of all sensation, save for its removal. Oblivion won't cut it – what's needed is its utter withdrawal, the structure of an abyss from which to howl, a language to frame tales that can be told only with a requisite distance from the events themselves.

Hilary is whispering under her breath, not to Lance, but to herself. To make sure she's still there. This can't be borne, all of this *everything,* the noise and colors. She can feel skin cells sloughing off, each individual molecule within each individual metabolic operation. She can smell the color of her eyes and hear her hair growing. She can see the rising breath of the assembled party, in hues as variable as the respective contents of their stomachs.

The twins feel the minivan arriving. They must do – they certainly can't *hear* it, its satin glide through buttery pavement. Their spread arms fall to their sides, and they beckon the next eight passengers, of whom Hilary and Lance make up a quarter. They no longer feel so attractive. Catching her reflection in the door as she moves towards it, Hilary is struck by the eviscerating effect the evening has had upon her cheeks and lips. Her face is chewed from the inside out, sucked back and inhaled, trampled and worn. Two yachting ropes hang down from either side of her head, element-ravaged despite the theatre's absolute insulation from the outside world. Lance matches her posture, hunched and rabbit-like, pushed from the shoulders into the chest, laden with the rigors of the night's loading. Lance takes a bit of time to unglue his arms from their locked position, in order to take the next step. He's rigid, still crossed; as though protecting his organs, or readying himself for burial.

At the very edge of the threshold, a step away from the outside, a twin hands them each a token. It's nothing special – a round of plastic coated with metallic paint – but there's an uncanny weight about it that suggests a potency not to be fucked with. Lance can't help but sneer with distaste at the trite symbols embossed into the surface. A leering comedy face on one side, a weeping death mask on the other, both entwined with ribbon. How cliché. He would have expected something a little more cerebral and sophisticated from the grand dame. But no matter, their purpose is clear.

Outside air hits the skin like a defibrillator paddle. All clench and thrum, and it becomes clearer to see why some passenger required help entering the vehicle. First, payment. The driver smells like greasepaint and aniseed, even in the open air.

The tokens chink heavy into the silver box, like the turning of a key in a heavy lock, kicking clockwork operations into action.

Hilary manages without help. She's taking the back seat, too paranoid to entertain the thought of anyone sitting behind her. Still smarting from the show, she knows one more stroke of contact will set her off beyond retrieval. She's never been a woman with much of a stomach for the damsel's wail, and this is not the place to start.

On automatic, Lance climbs in behind her, still jerking his limbs as though they don't belong to him. He takes pains to maintain a respectable distance between them, thighs repulsing like two magnets of twin polarity.

Cityscape blurs, a carousel of overpasses and sodium-strobed tunnels, interspersed with Little Chefs and the occasional nest of roadside sculptures. The passengers in front are dropped off in pairs, from the city center out to the suburbs. Eventually Hilary and Lance are the only ones remaining. It seems to take longer to reach their destinations than those of their predecessors, the tension between the two slapping thick layers of emulsion over each passing instant. Only when the vehicle eventually pulls up in front of Lance's semi does Hilary realize that they're way off course for her own flat.

The driver says nothing; like before, he exits the front, stalks around to open the passenger door, and stands waiting. Lance invests nothing in a farewell, save for,

"See you later. Sort out any money stuff next time I see you."

Unfolding himself from the minivan, he stiffens at the sensation of eyes still fixed on his neck, the back of his head. All too bare. *Bitch*, he thinks, and it fails to catch. The word feels strange, unfamiliar, puppet-mouthed – it wasn't working. He'll have to work harder on hating her.

Hilary remains proper as a doily, hands on opposite knees, calves thrust upward and pert from the balls of her feet. The driver stares at her, or seems to – his blank face a mirror of her own, and he stands motionless at the open door. The frost of incoming dew wraps itself around her neck, inching down her shoulders. She shivers. Searching her inventory for an appropriate way to address the wraith, she turns down the notches on her impending shrillness, switching to the tactical voice of reason employed in the boardroom, in department stores.

"Sir, this isn't my stop. I stay in Cheravon Wynd, back toward the West End."

Dry fog, skeletal leaves and alkali-smoking hiss a reply.

"No questions. No comments. Last stop."

All without an incline of the head on the neck, without shifting a hand from the door. A voice incapable of debate, no nuance with which to negotiate. Lance believes his sister may have found her match. Sunlight tinges the eastern horizon a mustard yellow. It's no longer practical to make demands.

"Just get out, Hilary. I'll take you home tomorrow."

She complies, if only to shift out from under the inspection of the faceless guard.

"Uh…thank you," she murmurs, always professional, and follows her brother up the gravel driveway to the front door. He's amazed to discover his keys in his pocket, where they'd remained all evening. It's bizarre to lay hands on this fragmentary evidence of the man he was twelve hours previously. A man with a house, an identity bound up with a name and a purpose.

This is simply it, here and now. The void is most obvious when it's looked into. Performance, intensity, bracketed by weaker counterparts of prologue and afterword. Hangover and regret as addendum, no explanatory notes required.

Now that the show is over, they no longer bleed viscera onto an empty stage, spread legs and diaries wide for the gaping crowds. All that remains behind is the garbage.

Lance circles the room like he's never seen it before. Suede-effect paint, paint-effect suede, fake drawer and cupboard fascia, pony-skin rugs, blind alleys. Illusion of space, illusion of light, illusion of depth, illusion of height. Every item and fixture conspiring to be something it is not. Hilary makes herself uncomfortable on the dusky leather ottoman – he doesn't mind, now: it doesn't seem to belong to him anymore.

She's drumming her fingernails on the coffee table, waiting for a conclusion to be reached as to what they're going to do next. He glares at it; an offensively trite fusion of chrome and glass. It's by Karl Lagerfeld – a name whose originality has become so bland that it's recognized even by the spellchecker on his computer. The polished salesperson in Jenners had informed him, with a perfectly straight face, that the item would change his life. He wishes now he'd never laid eyes upon it. Its purchase filled the dead time of a card transaction, its delivery the opening of a door. Just part of the landscape, imparting no clues as to the nature of the buyer.

They play duets in paltry strains, submerged in the clamour of the entire orchestra. A father. A few genes. A proclivity for mind-altering substances, specifically those with the power of elevation over and above their wretched selves. The recognition that they possess the ability to repulse others; so entirely, that they find solace only in each other. All the while loathing each bone and cell in the other body.

They are easily pleased and easily appeased when the layers are peeled back. When stuffed with yellow, with red pushing up between skin and entrails, there's nothing explosive for the drugs to rub up against save for the dearth of sensation that's already there. The thick, black, noxious nothing swallows anything that comes within reach.

"We're a pair of...fucking...*black holes*," mumbles Lance, grabbing at the nearest idiom gleaned from cult television.

"Speak for yourself."

The only thing keeping them present is the satisfaction taken from scratching the freshness from healing scars, too tired to sniff out fresh blood.

"Fuck, Lance. How often have we decided to cut this shit?"

They've been here before, albeit on a smaller scale, a gentler fall from a lower altitude. Like so many gone before, they've tried as many clean-up operations as they have intoxicants. Detoxification becomes retoxification, too many ketones swirling around for the body to cope with, too many divisions for the mind to enclose.

Hilary swallows glossy magazine articles like vitamins. Read voraciously over liquid lunches; some unvoiced hope in the power of osmosis by virtue of proximity.

Each suggestion merits a try, having the Vogue or Cosmopolitan stamp of approval, but all inevitably lead back to a variation on an original theme. Detox drinks paved the way for diet pills, progressing rather naturally onto stackers. Meditation eventually called for a few joints with which to open the mind; it was never dark enough. Barring solid carbohydrates from the diet necessitated the augmentation of her alcohol intake, in order to quell hunger pangs.

Lance relies on his charity standing orders to offset any specklings of guilt inherent in the carbon footprint and sweatshop derivation of a pair of shoes, a new suit. Herbal remedies avail him nothing but strange smells and discoloured urine. On his bosses' suggestion, he attends primal scream therapy; a course of sessions designed for bellowing out corporate discontents. He succeeds in rupturing a vessel in his throat, which at least apportions a legitimate reason for any blood-coughing, as opposed to the consequences of smoking industrial cleanser.

They both try religion, early on, part of their inheritance from their father. Hilary takes prescription anti-depressants from both her NHS general practitioner and private healthcare provider. Nothing works, of course.

They still leave too many fingerprints, too many credit trails, for oblivion to ever really work. Polly's drug is not a magic potion; it works only so far as the goalposts and arm-lengths of numbness or of riotous sensitivity hold steady. This is never for long enough to mean anything; they drift further and further apart. The trick lies in the expositional over the pharmaceutical – with all acts and reactions exposed, bathed under the spotlight, the subjects are more real and present than they ever can be when moving in spheres surreptitiously dictated by gurus and experts. The confessions generate an incomparable high – simply by dragging hidden facets out for all to see, those secrets the soul's cipher, broken down into the elementary. It's never enough to be, to exist, to float in a bubble alongside recollections, with their appended guilt, fear, iniquity or distaste. Memory must speak. It must be captured, heard, eaten, drunk, snorted, sucked and fucked and pumped with formaldehyde, preserved forever in swollen plasticity as a validation of a life lived instead of consumed, endured.

The best part of the process was trying it all over again, just to make sure the relics don't lie. It's easy enough; now, more than ever, it's on all sides. It sits before, between, inside, astride. Minds may be lost, limits may be tested beyond repair, but the thrill of a loaded weapon is an arm they can't resist bearing.

Lance loses patience, striding to a cupboard door in a gold-leaf-painted recess in the corner of the room. He throws the door open with a no regard for the impacted wall. Dragging sheets, pillowslips, eiderdowns, bolsters and duvet covers from the depths in a frenzy, he's soon knee-deep in a drift of Egyptian cotton. When the shelves are bare, and he leans upon them, panting, like a small child checking for closet monsters. There's nothing in there but dust bunnies and the occasional corpse-sticky spiders' web – certainly no answers, nothing to stem the flow of questions.

"What are you doing?" Hilary asks, idly, too preoccupied with the study of her chipped fingernail polish to devote much attention to the answer.

"Digging a hole. Building a dry-stane dyke. What the fuck does it look like?"

"Looks like a mess, bro."

"I'm making up the couch. You can have my room." He avoids the three-letter word, allowing the blanks to express themselves. Hilary doesn't want to sleep in his bed if he's not there. Nothing more disaffecting than the scent of another without the accompanying warmth…she can't bear the thought of cooling aftershave, fossilizing sweat.

"No, I'll take the couch."

There's no point in much argument either way. The sun is rising, sleep is another country. Lance deposits a handful of bedding, now a crumpled armful of wild disarray, onto the arm of the sofa.

"Fine. You know where everything is."

Lance turns, kicking off his shoes. They skate across the hardwood, perpetrating his status as an invisible man, moving around outside of his former self. He slinks towards the stairs, Hilary calls,

"Shouldn't we talk about this?"

"There's nothing to talk about. Nothing to say that hasn't already been said."

Hilary can't quite figure out where her outrage has gone, the vengeful pride that typically characterizes such dawn-frazzled dismissals. Quiet now. It seems strange that there's no need for a scrap of paper, a phone number scrawled in eyeliner pencil. It's all too personal, perverted familiarity. Conventions left behind somewhere; on the taxi floor, in the lobby, in the bathroom, in the recent past, a smear, an echo.

"Okay. I'll be off as soon as it's daytime proper. Should I wake you?"

"Don't bother."

Lance sees no point in perpetuating the illusion that this is some fucking country and western ballad. He'd laugh if it weren't so horrendous.

Hilary begins strewing sheets about the couch, on automatic, knowing she'll be wide-eyed for days to come. She remembers something. A pixellated face, a digitized set of numbers, a smell of rusted piping.

"Lance?"

He stops once more, hackles raised, still facing the stairs.

"*What?!*" His practiced modulation and careful articulation has gone, sending consonants trickling airlessly down his throat.

"I don't have any money for a taxi home. I don't get paid till the weekend. Could you lend me a few quid until then?"

Lance begins to snicker, first in a stunted breath, then a crackle of dead leaves. His shoulders heave with misplaced mirth as he attempts to unite concerns of utter disparity. Like discovering he's down to his last cigarette whilst watching a razed village bow under a mushroom cloud. He unbuckles his belt, whips it through the loops, and tosses it to the floor with a snaky hiss. Keeping his back to Hilary, he fumbles open the top button on his trousers, and jerks them over his backside and down his legs with a furious tug. The left side won't co-operate, and he stands on one empty leg then the other, lifting his knees and stamping, until freed, like a dancing dervish. The garment, finally detached, slumps in rebuke. He slides it across the floor towards Hilary with a boot of revulsion.

"There's money in there. Should be plenty. God knows I owe you one."

She grabs the end of a trouser leg and draws the article toward her, slowly, petting an animal that may bite if provoked.

"Thanks, Lance."

"No, sister dear. Thank *you*."

He doesn't bother drawing in any of the venom from his voice. Keeping up the momentum from the evening, letting it all out into the open, sliding down his chest and across the floor. He still can't bear to turn and look, watching the mocking daybreak sketch mocking haloes around her head. Nature's lighting effects and costume changes have never been so colorlessly apt.

It's bizarre. Now that it's out there in the relative open, hanging naked from the catwalks and pelmets of the theatre, there's no need any more for pretence.

The promise of anonymity rings truer in these circumstances than any other – bound together by a shared truth, the other audience members will no more spill the dirt than scream their own dirty secrets from the top of the nearest tower-block. One for one, like at school. All the classified information teeters like a Jenga tournament, strapping them into a protracted Russian roulette.

The confusion remains as to the purpose of the exercise. For Polly it may be as simple as pure art. Channeling the disconcerting elements of counter-cinema to riotous effect…the compulsion to study car-crashes, watch autopsies, pick scabs.

There appears no charitable manifesto, no offer of rehabilitation – just the rogues' gallery. Audience gathered at the foot of the gallows, grinning at the streams of piss and drawn-off pride running down the legs of the criminals.

They don't even yell the way they used to. Once upon a time, the roof would buck and rear to the sound of the roaring crowd, baying for blood. Nowadays they hiss and titter, the whispered cluck of disapproval – not yet accustomed to the drawing back of curtains, as opposed to the furtive peek from between the netting.

Perhaps it's the overarching accord that, when it came down to judgment, screaming at inanimate objects can't abolish them. No point in clawing at porcelain and wax; more effigies will shore up to replace them.

They grow, too, without interference, like gardens run wild with ivy and dandelions. They're supposed to drift upwards, merely burning holes in the ozone layer. Instead, the clouds of iniquity drop seeds and spores into waiting ears. Portraying the atrocities has one of two immediate effects, but eventually they coalesce into a single impulse – the craving for more of the same, now, again, evermore. The first and most natural is repulsion. A great shining scarlet circle in which the sinners and reprobates move around in the act, or retell it through tears of forced penitence, barred across the middle with a belt of prohibition. Initially, the thought performing or reliving the exploits is horrifying enough to halt the thrust of impulse. The shaking of heads and chirps of disapproval sends the witnesses thrumming like a hornet's nest.

But the seeds are planted, the concepts are introduced, the hot primal blood stirs from that hidden place within. The desire to see more, hear more, feel the same scrape of knives on flesh as slices of exterior are stripped to reveal more of the lowest lows. Dirt can be filthier, bones can rattle louder, blood can be thicker and darker than that which has been seen already.

Dramatizing the actions has the unfortunate side-effect of eventually rending it legitimate, even acceptable. The unpeeling layers release buds of scent, ripple satiny sheen as they hit the floor. Familiar, comfortable, and suddenly attractive.

Suddenly there's no harm in trying it out – the worst that can happen is up there for all to see. Acknowledging impulses can't curb them indefinitely – worse, it often has the reverse effect, diluting the distaste of the incident, making it more palatable.

Hilary and Lance find themselves in the eye, now idols, raised and fallen in equal measure. They can no longer root and hurt, steal or exploit, fight and fuck in peace, with a head-full of air. Others have entered the microcosm of their arrangement. Taste and touch of skin and hair is now bracketed between the velvet drapes. Never having been keen on looking into each other's eyes, they now must face the staring out of myriad others.

And they won't stop, they can't stop, despite their self-deception in the immediate aftermath. There is nothing left to lose: it's all out there now, anyway.

Part X

Carrie awakens to the strangest of sounds – like the center of a collapsing galaxy, a rebelling garbage disposal unit with a mouthful of spent bullets. Pushing the duvet aside, without first checking whether the sunlight hits the room at a dangerous level of brilliance, she jerks from the bed and wrenches open the bedroom door.

It's coming from downstairs, the hallway. A drift of chill lancing across her bare feet indicates that the front door is wide open, allowing the outside in.

The wrenching howls are peppered with small pauses, indicating their emanation from a respiring organism. It's got to be Tracy – but the sound she makes is unlike anything Carrie could have imagined.

"Mum?" she calls, warily. "Is that you?"

The wailing ceases abruptly for a moment, before resuming once more, interrupted with the shaky drawing of breath as Tracy tries to calm herself down. Carrie refuses to move from her position of safety, inside her own room, until she hears an intelligible word or phrase. Finally,

"Aye, sweetheart."

"What's wrong?"

A series of hisses and clicks rumbles out, like the prelude to an answering machine recording, as Tracy gulps sense into her discourse.

"Nothing, hen. Just a bit of a mess, I'll sort it."

Tracy and mess, particularly its resolution, strung up illogical concepts across the ceiling of the household. Coupled with the inhuman keening from the hallway, there's definitely something up.

Carrie prepares herself for leaving her sanctuary, wrapping up in a terrycloth bathrobe and a pair of moth-eaten cartoon-deco slippers, shaking her head to free it from fuzz and bring it back into the room in which she stands.

Then she proceeds, screwing up her eyes against the incoming reality jolt. Crossing the landing, she catches her reflection in the mirror. Not a pretty sight – hair a birds' nest indicative of some pillow-wrestling calisthenics, pale skin showing up piss-holes for eyes and dark bruising on each elbow from leaning on the bar for the best part of the evening. She's probably deficient in something; should eat more thoughtfully instead of mainlining cocktail cherries as meal replacements.

She reaches the top of the stairs and gazes down at the back of her mother's head. Tracy sits on the bottom step, arms wrapped around her torso, rocking slightly back and forth, from more than the chill from the front door.

Framed in the doorway is a mound of sparkling glass, arranged (or perhaps deranged) around and across the doormat, strafed artfully with shreds of green plastic bin-bag. Broken bottles, all having held various kinds of alcohol. It's a nature reserve of frolicking intoxicants – green, red, brown, amber, blue shells of wine, beer, gin, vodka, schnapps, and all recent inhabitants of Tracy's fridge and drinks cabinet. There's so many of them she can't count, can't distinguish one from another in the cause of a vague estimate. Then, it's not the number; it's the significance of their presence outside the front door. It's a message from the fucking Neighborhood Watch, or whatever such a faction amounts to in this decrepit satellite town.

"Aw, mum!" Carrie thunders downstairs, bouncing off the hall carpet and throwing her arms around her mother's shoulder. Only as she feels the tremors, scents a frisson of Elizabeth Arden mixed with Gordon's gin, does she realize she hasn't been this close up to her mother in what seems like years. She's lost weight. Going by the length of shadow on the lawn – shortish, can't be that far past noon – and the sharp freshness of the alcohol, she's drinking in the morning again.

"It's them…fucking *bastards* from across the way," Tracy whimpers, dropping her head into her hands. It takes Carrie a moment or two to translate, but she understands immediately. Action was required.

"Right, come on, come through and sit down. I'll take care of this." She doesn't expect an argument, and doesn't get one – Tracy's still in the pliant stage of her inebriety, well off the energy boost that accompanies her tolerance threshold.

As she parks her mother on the couch, and makes for the kitchen in search of heavy gloves and plastic bags, she runs through the probable sequence of events.

Those bottles are from the back green. Each of the houses on the scheme looks out onto a shared quadrangle, over the rear fence of each property. Purportedly for washing lines and Argos swing sets, it was, in reality, a nuclear wasteland of abandoned shopping carts, wheelbarrows full of decaying stuffed animals, dead household appliances, mutilated bicycles, ripped tyres and enough razor-wire chest-height serge to thwart visibility of any goings-on in the yard after dark. Even the goopy-eyed lap dogs - of which many of the older residents were fond - refused to void their innards in the badlands, preferring to skitter in their short-legged fragility further afield to the park.

Since Carrie could remember, it had been a game of buried treasure between her father and herself to cart the evidence of her parents' alcohol consumption out to the back green. Her father had tried to explain it away, when she became old enough to question the purpose of playing pirate.

"See they big bins we have? Well, see now that we're a family with a nice house and nice things, we don't have enough room for all our rubbish. So what we do is put them out the back for just now, until they give us an even bigger bin."

Carrie hadn't been convinced – she'd been told about litter, and its proper place, at school, and she didn't want her dad to get into trouble.

"But dad, it's dropping rubbish, it's wrong. It's going to smell, and the teacher says rats and beasties come and get you when you leave litter."

Carrie's father had smiled indulgently, patted her on the head and said,

"Don't you worry about that, darling. Rats and beasties only look for rubbish that has bits ay food in it, don't they? The bottles are just fine back there, cause they're made ay glass, and glass don't melt in the rain and get all smelly, the way rubbish does. You see what I mean?"

Carrie knew better than to argue, and didn't want to put her dad in a bad mood.

"Yes, dad. I suppose so. So I won't get into trouble?"

Frank jammed his hands into her armpits, tickled her quickly, then hoisted her into the air, spinning her around the room at arm's

97

length. She squealed and begged to be let down, with enough of a pleasurable giggle in her voice to indicate that she wanted nothing of the sort. She loved it when her father played properly; he rarely had time. He placed her gently on the ground, and said,

"Darling, you'll never get into trouble unless it's off me, and I know all your tickly spots. But I tell you what: how about we find another game for the garden? No more bottles, just in case."

Her old man never asked her to drop litter again. That afternoon, he'd taught her to play hopscotch, numbers etched into the slabs with a sharp rock. She'd gradually forgotten about the bottles, which did periodically decimate on their own as a result of her father's infrequent trips to the dump. After he'd gone, she'd forgotten about the old secret, her parent's old habit. Until now, the evidence at her feet a clear indication that her mother was nowhere near as assiduous as her father when it came to managing the pile-up.

The initial planning of the satellite towns was to create communities, as opposed to neat rows of glorified clapboard mausoleums. It worked at first – loads of first-time homeowners and retirees, generally happy to give each other peace. The American picket-fence idealism is anathema to the discerning Scottish villager; warm apple pies and backyard barbecues practically the stuff of nightmares. Still, having little by way of entertainment, and even less by way of wall-space between houses, meant that the kids produced grew up to be bored and antisocial little shits, with nothing better to do than cause havoc. The upshot of this is the growing value apportioned to idle gossip. Nobody talks much to each other, but that doesn't mean the neighbours don't make for frequent subject matter, derided and criticized in snide intonations over the breakfast table. That intrinsic need to have one over on everyone else, even just a little, is magnified and distorted out of all proportion in the lack of anything else to talk about. Curtains twitched at nameless faces, weeds on the front lawn rustling with faceless names.

Fucking bastards, the whole lot of them. Think they're upwardly mobile now that they've got their Sky Plus Digibox, their broadband, their prissy little cars on higher purchase. Reckon they've got it cinched with their vandal-proof masonry paint and steering wheel clamps, their knock-off Thai replica Louis Vuitton handbags, their shipments of booze from across the Channel. Never mind that they're still living in the back of beyond, that they're kidding themselves on that there's anything out here except junk, shit, tarmac, concrete and more shit. They've got a cracking piece of civilian up-man-ship with Tracy here. She's managed to stay clear of too much scrutiny in the absence of a pregnant teen or a pending court appearance adding spice to the household – but she's still a fucking alky, and they're not going to let her away with that one easily. That's hot news, elevated by the small-town gossips to the dimensions of a circus sideshow, even if it only holds their attention for as long as it takes to spill a bin-bag of booze bottles all over the porch. As far as artistic expression goes, it's way too obvious and painfully mundane – like painting swastikas on a household of German residents, or littering the lawns of the morbidly obese with fast food wrappers. Grabbing onto flimsy symbols, in no way scratching deeper into the lives of the pariah du jour.

Perhaps this is the embodiment of the community spirit the town planners were aiming for – in disseminating the less favourable traits of certain residents, creating for them tawdry reputations, the perpetrators unite in their self-generated superiority.

Carrie is irritated by the prick of hurt pressing in at her stomach as she bags the shards. This idiocy may be below her on a level that's purely cerebral, but that can't annihilate entirely the human desire for acceptance. The glass strewing the porch is an unsubtle and unnecessary statement of malevolence, disgust: sharp shards slicing away any show of coherence and normality that Tracy's tried to maintain since Frank left. In spite of her care, even with the heavy gloves on Carrie receives a few thorny slashes from the shambles. The edges glint in the afternoon sunlight, winking in mockery. Carrie glares, remembering her father's consolation. It's unfortunate he's not here, for her to win the old argument. Although glass can't rot or stink, by its nature it casts a permanent glazing over the wreckage it comprises.

The porch is cleared without comment. She chokes back a furious sob at the vandals' unwarranted act of cruelty against people they know nothing about, that they clearly abhor for no reason other than having somebody to torture. Tracy may be a lot of things, but she doesn't deserve this cowardly declaration of a silent war. Carrie knows she can hold her own in a fight if and when it came down to it, and the lack of a face to pin this on is giving her a headache, clenching her jaw, grinding her teeth.

On the other side of the city, in West Brunswick, a nicer village with an official Neighborhood Watch team, Evan shuffles papers in his bedroom and nurses a pint of black coffee. He has an assignment due for university in the week to come, and for the first time in his academic career he's been procrastinating. There were books to acquire from the library, articles to annotate, topic sentences to construct around a paragraph plan he's not yet written. The question posed, to be answered by the essay, examines the relationship between the popular media and the subjects portrayed, contrasting reputable broadsheets with lewd, crude monosyllabic redtops. It looked simple enough last week – *broadsheets good, proper new. Redtops bad, gossip and scare mongering. Repeat to the tune of two thousand words.* He stands by the overview, but somehow things don't seem so simple anymore. Two days into his city job, he'd expected a cultural reawakening. Instead, he's oddly diverted from the arts by the prospect of another shift, and another round of quiet drinks with Carrie.

The answers to the essay question are located in several of the books on the recommended reading list. Large paragraphs outlining and disparaging throwaway trash media droop from between inverted commas on several lecture handouts. He doesn't know why he has to regurgitate the answers back at the lecturers, particularly in response to such a blindingly foregone conclusion.

There's no magic, nor discovery, in the exercise. Nothing spins, trapped in a gravity bypass, throwing blinding spears of light onto the pages.

Evan glances at the room around him. His walls are pasted with Esquire and GQ centerfolds, rock posters given gratis with copies of NME and Kerrang. His CD and DVD collections are equally pedestrian, mostly carried over from high school and the occasional glance at the student union newspaper. He throws the pile of papers to the floor, stands up and takes a closer look. Throwing open his wardrobe, he can barely account for his own tastes in any of the items hanging within – with a blush creeping even in his solitude, he realizes most of the articles are courtesy of shopping trips with his mum. Five black T-shirts, five white, two plaid shirts, various tops printed with logos from bands he could care less about, four pairs of jeans, two black suits, one pinstriped, and nothing with any thread of personality whatsoever. No lovingly repaired lucky trousers, no frayed shirt-sleeves, no paint spatters or discolored laundry casualties. All interchangeable, clean, neat, bereft.

A flashback. High school. Barely two years ago, but it feels like a lifetime. School uniforms were implemented in fourth year to combat the increasingly violent altercations between factions of pupils, whose militant attire marked out allies and enemies. The gangsters beat on the trendies, the trendies beat on the footballers, the footballers beat on the Goths, and the Goths cried and cut themselves up. The faculty's solution to the problem was to try their utmost to make everybody the same – cue black trousers and skirts cut firmly below the knee, white long-sleeved shirts, pert black navy-style blazers and a tie striped in migraine-provoking purple and green. Evan complied, of course. Now, though, he's stuck through with regrets at having accepted the garb at face value, no arguments or murmurs of dissent. He remembers the ways in which pupils wrested their individual quirks from the depths of their penguin suits. Button, badges, necklaces, stitched-on ribbons, patches...and that was just on the blazers. Millinery and luggage, footwear and hosiery opened up whole new worlds of self-expression. It's interesting now to note the creativity employed under such a regime – and sad to realize he'd never bothered to try himself, mostly because he wasn't sure what kind of statements he could issue. He closes the wardrobe doors and perches on the end of the bed, knees twitching from the balls of his restless feet.

It's the cause of no end of frustration that this doesn't seem to be getting any clearer. He feels too old now to be reborn in an image of his own making. That's the kind of thing he should have sorted at school – picked a subset and stuck with it, learned the ways and rites and fashions of his chosen clan. Now he's still a blank canvas, but one which the passage of time seems to be slowly removing of potential for painting. An existential dilemma at the age of nineteen is, of course, ahead of its time, but to him it already feels too late. Almost as though he's missed a fecund point in his development, lost the instruction manual along the way, and consequently stands clueless in borrowed clothes and borrowed tastes. A mimic, a fraud, without the ebullient characteristics of any given imitated subject to create a parody worth a second look. He floats past, an extra in the movie of his own life, if such a trite allegory could ever stand up to any interrogation.

Up until now, there's always been his studies. Correct answers, incorrect answers, accurately appropriated concepts and a bushel of single letters, stringing out across his landscape like road-signs along Sesame Street. It's easier to rhyme off grades as an appraisal of accomplishments than to scrape for measures of success and experience requiring any further description.

Now the academic rigor begins to pall, as holes appear in the fabric of the manifesto, like cigarette burns through a lampshade. There's more – there's nothing in these sheets and studies commending the majesty of a teenage sorceress, tossing cocktails shakers through the air, moving in her own field of electricity. There's nothing about defying the laws of gravity, nothing questioning the cultural or artistic significance of a pair of flaming orange eyes, and nothing to explain why he feels drawn to and inspired by these phenomena beyond the quantifiable. He briefly entertains the notion that he may be falling in love: but quickly dismisses it as an explanation too simple to attach to something he can't quite get his aching head around. He hears too many classmates at university attribute the word to dalliances that amount to little more than a wine-soaked honeymoon period, characterized by laborious sex tournaments and a fusion around the hip area, and followed up by a series of awkward avoidant glances between the exes and death-flirting drinking binges. This *thing*, whatever it was, doesn't fit the blueprint. More than that; Carrie, the theatre, the unpeeled frivolity in the bar – it attacks the senses in such a revelatory manner as to stand apart from the all-encompassing blindness of love.

Besides, there's no real evidence yet. He hasn't noticed any particular changes in his sleeping pattern or eating habits, and he's tossing off no more nor less than usual. Carrie appears in too many fragments to be united and absorbed as an object of unfettered adoration. The usual suspects – eyes, teeth, hair, hands, voice – are mixed up with the less specific traits, pieces of scenery and prop, which stand meaningless alone. The past two evenings shutter-click past too rapidly to analyze for proper responses, probable causes.

Evan groans, lolls his head around on his stiffened neck, and tips back, draining his eyeballs into the back of his skull. Clearly, today will not be a productive one in terms of study. His head's too full of nonsense, packed with polystyrene balls, which squeak inanities and forever shift him from coherent thought. He stares into the depths of the coffee mug on the floor. The cooling contents now glisten with traces of washing-up liquid, spilling treacle rainbows across his reflection in the surface. Like her hair. Fuck, he's turning into one of *them*. Pavlovian triggers everywhere, or worse – maybe he's actively looking for them without admitting it to himself. There's no such thing as a happy accident – it's all courtesy of the remarkable human ability to extort significance from the most inconsequential observations. He wishes he had the stomach to quell such uprisings with something stronger. Stretching back onto the bed, clacking his vertebrae and spreading his arms, he waits, like Carrie, for nightfall.

Part XI

This is a spinning coin, right enough. Hilary sits on the wrong side of the desk, on the wrong side of the morning. At the side of the room, looking over all, Cathy smirks, an expression her marshmallow face shouldn't, by all rights, be able to support.

Jensen is not a happy man in general, but today, a gliding light takes the edge off his misery – the opportunity to give a staff member a righteous and thorough bollocking. He places his elbows on the desk and shifts around in the leather swing chair, seeking bouncier expanses of seating as yet unexhausted by his twin-tub rear. Having thoroughly suffocated every inch with his blubbery backside, he unearths a sigh from the depths of his chest, and fans out a sheaf of papers onto the desk.

"Ms Carntyne," he begins, stretching the buzz of the title with the contempt he believes it deserves, "This is unacceptable."

Cathy nods slowly, under the erroneous impression it imbues her with professional dignity. Hilary waits for it. She doesn't particularly care what's coming; everything still waves through the hyper-bright lens of insomnia.

"Would you like to begin with your explanation as to what on earth you thought you were doing?" asks Jensen.

"I gave Cathy an assignment. I thought she'd enjoy having a bit of freedom."

Jensen squares again, in as much as his rounded contours will allow.

"Indeed. That may be true, but it's simply *not* the way we do things here. We have a set of codes, regulations and work ethics, and going over the heads of the management is not permitted. Do you realize that Cathy has been working on this…*assignment*…for the better part of a straight twenty-four hours? She's contracted for a maximum of seven point five per day. This has wide and serious implications for the payroll staff, the trade union regulations, fire safety in the event of an evacuation. And that's before we even come to the data protection, privacy and plagiarism regulations that your intern has inadvertently broken, without having been informed by either yourself or another senior staff member."

Jensen enjoys using big words almost as much as Cathy. They must have had a ball, whipping up a storm of bureaucratic jargon with which to skewer Hilary's lapses in judgement. Fortunately for them, she's lacking somewhat in the energy required to counter their arguments. She settles for some gloss.

"Look, I'm sorry I overstepped the mark. Cathy's been paying close attention to what I do. Very enthusiastic. It seemed a shame to keep her stuck in secretarial stuff when she could have…I don't know, spread her wings a little."

This tactic of shifting focus often worked in the boardroom. Turning every action into a favour, every mistake into someone else's, is a time-honoured tactic.

It doesn't work. Derision drips in glistening droplets from Jensen's bald head, all over the papers on the desk. Gathering his chins about him, he tips his head back, guffawing.

"I've been in this business since before you were born. I know your kind only too well – you'll do anything for an easy time of it. You were irresponsible and you know it: I also have my doubts as to your dedication to the tasks at hand. These were left under the hood of your scanner."

He gathers the papers and hands them to Hilary. Shit. She'd stuffed them away in a hurry. It wasn't what the sheets said, it was what they *didn't* – reams of professional copy defaced with her manic morning scrawl. It looked pretty bad. Prophetic: like that bit in *The Shining* when Jack Torrance types the same thing over and over and over again as a symptom of his disintegrating psyche. All work and no play makes Jack a dull boy, certainly, but the coded messages in Hilary's sloping italic were more unsettling by virtue of their incomprehensibility.

Bag it up. Take it out. I hate you. What's your name? More not less. Can't make words, gorge inside, a gulf. So predictable. Fuck this shit this is nonsense losing my mind losing my mind!!! Green green green yellow yellow yellow lorry red red yellow lorry red red red…

Scribbles in red pen, green pen, thick Magic Marker – spirals, boxes, phone numbers which, had Jensen cared to check, would have put him onto her erstwhile dealer. Hilary feels an unfamiliar, long-forgotten blush of shame crawling from her shirt collar. This wasn't good.

"Would you care to explain yourself? You appear to have been wasting company time on these…artistic endeavours," Jensen spits.

"I…don't know…" she trails off, bombast and negotiation dying in her throat. "I've been under a bit of strain lately. Family trouble."

"And it's affecting your work?" A redundant question. Then, before allowing her to answer, "There's clearly more at work here than the grave shirking of responsibility. I think you'd better go home for the rest of the week. Come in on Monday and report to me. I'm not going to suspend you, yet, but I want to hear an impressive case as to why I should keep you on in this company. Your behaviour has been unacceptable, and we both need some time to think about where to go from here."

For the first time in as long as she can remember, Hilary has been caught at it without a get-out. She nods, conceding defeat.

"Yes, Mr Jensen. I'm sorry. I'll be back on Monday."

She stands, adjusting her head to fit the new downward glance to which she's becoming accustomed, and leaves the room. She walks into her office in a daze, glancing around at the drywalled torture chamber. In the bottom drawer of her desk; a small lockable petty cash tin. Not enough in there for anything top-class, but enough to delay the dawn of reason for a few days. Staring at the floor, taking the stairs instead of the elevator, she checks out of the building, this time officially.

The drive home passes in a flash. She stops at traffic lights with more caution than usual, captivated now by the flaring gems and their power over conduct.

Her only other pit-stop on the way is the Peckhams wine store on Glassford Street. There's a sign on the window advertising a ten percent discount on purchases of six bottles or more, and it seems a shame not to take advantage. Six bottles of wine probably wouldn't cut it for the whole weekend, but it's enough for now.

A trail of shoes, handbag, blazer, briefcase paves the way from the front door of her apartment to the kitchen. There, she grabs a wineglass and a corkscrew and retreats to her bedroom for as long as it

106

will take to feel completely adrift from the rest of the planet. Her first instinct is to call Lance, but that's no longer an option, not now. Settling for her own company is rendered a little more palatable when she notes the benefits to be had from talking to oneself. She gets only the answers she wants to hear, to the questions that only she is prepared to ask. Plus, she wouldn't have to share the wine.

It's three in the afternoon. Hilary draws the curtains to block out the light, and is suddenly grateful for the urban clutter bricking the view. Here, the bedroom is hamstrung from the height of sunshine by the building opposite. She creaks the wine open and luxuriates in the mountain-spring splash of liquid on glass. Before the first sip, she shakes out the satin eiderdown topping her leather-boarded king-size bed, lovingly smoothing her patch of comfort for the evening ahead.

The television on the opposite wall is a possibility entertained only for a moment. It's not the time for yet more forced sparkle, and she's got the dreadful feeling she'd only be searching for soap-stories that matched her own. Her bedside table is stacked with books, but she can't face the task of contorting combinations of words into images in her head – there's no space. Grabbing a matchbox-sized remote control, she presses PLAY and transforms the room into a cabin of sound.

She splays out on the bed at an angle fiercely calculated to maintain the level of wine in the glass, and drowns in a spectrum of pitch and chord. Bass licks at the undersurface of the bed. Somnolent piano strokes and chiming guitars dance up and down the walls, tracing shapes. Drumrolls and rattling snare barricade her further into her own head, where it's both safely impenetrable and dangerously volatile.

She remembers the pleasure garnered from decorating this room, her first in a home of her own. Nobody to please but herself, no compromises required. She'd gone for red and gold, to match her nails and hair. It had always seemed so wonderfully decadent, crimson walls and golden drapes promising riches, the colour of the center of the earth. Now the ceiling collapses down around her under the weight of the textures. The mood lighting works only to obscure, hiding her from herself. The shadows serve to limit oracular access to the deepening crevices of her body, to press into the vacant and searching canyons in her mind.

She skitters idly through the pages of a glossy magazine, trying to remember a time when she cared about clothing and household goods for what they were, as opposed to an expensive distraction, a futile endeavor to make herself more acceptable. The only thing that satisfies her has the unfortunate side-effect of being the root of much of her misery. She recalls that old chestnut about hurt, probably read in the pages of the same publication currently strewing her pillow. *You always hurt the one you love.* She and Lance have never framed this aphorism more succinctly than in this interminable act of self-harm.

Only the moments in the midst of the chaos came close to countering the agony of the aftermath. Glistening purity, pared sensation, the melding of twin cravings and flesh on flesh, chromosome to chromosome.

Then came: the bathing, the scratching, the burning, cauterizing, medicating, all painful and pointless, and leading back around the circumference of the insanity for another hit. Torn between the noise in the head and the itch in the gut, the gut won out – the only outcome worse than the act was the possibility of a curtain falling forever over it all. Hilary spends hours afterwards castigating them both, proclaiming never to have wanted what she gets, but never allowing much to stand in the way of getting what she wants.

It's now six o'clock, hours swallowed up in the creeping twilight. The paint on the walls clots with darkness, dripping down the ceiling in the attic of the mind.

The rules have changed. It's only when he's past the front door, left unlocked as usual, and halfway up the stairs, does he sense that perhaps he should have buzzed the flat first. Now he's picking his way past chipped cement, cave-painting graffiti, gagging on the stench of stale piss, ascending to a reckoning. Old habits die hard; he steps up his pace, as eager as ever to escape the gloaming in the close.

He has a red in his pocket, and two in his eye sockets. He hasn't slept for what may as well be a week. Nothing solid has passed his lips since lunch at work, days before.

The door to her flat is open, too. He pauses, listens, and steps across the threshold, waiting, perhaps, for an alarm to sound. She's going to need a spell, a blockage.

Something to rescind his vampiric freedom in coming and going, something stronger and harder than willpower alone. He's come replete with drastic measures in any case – a stake through the heart, a garlic-stuffed beheading or immolation wouldn't be pushing it much further.

The hallway is darker than usual, shadows stretching out to accommodate his progress. The building is new enough to withdraw echoes from the floors and ceilings. Cement below thick carpeting absorbs his footsteps as he makes his way to the living room. He clicks the light on, then quickly off again, the sudden illumination thrumming like an anvil-blow through his delicate skull. She's not there. He tracks her trail of outerwear to the kitchen, where the sideboard cupboards and drawers lie ajar, attesting to the removal of drinking paraphernalia.

Bedroom, then, as all roads invariably lead. A nudge provides enough of an aperture to confirm that the darkness prevails in here, too. A stereo rings out from the corner, its blue screen the only light source. The door doesn't creak at all, of course, soaked and greased with WD40. Not like their parent's place. There's nothing like the sense of being perpetually undercover in your own home to instill a horror for the incidental, a distaste for unnecessary sights and sounds. Too loaded. Paranoid enough.

"Hil?"

A strangled reply. The music is turned down.

"I'm here."

Here. No more pointed a word for inscribing a moment, a feeling, the oft regrettable spontaneity of a drunken tattoo. Here in a time, a place. Here on the other end of the phone, at roll call at school. Here as simply not there, not elsewhere, not moving, no clause with which to escape.

There was the other, the older, the wiser, the attempt to transplant the self from the tightening confinement to a wider sphere of influence.

They both thought it'd get easier when they were grownups – whatever that meant. With freedom from home and independent lifestyles, there would come an influx of new and interesting faces, places, people. It worked the way quick fixes always do – for the moment and no further. In many ways it became more difficult. All those new things , added responsibilities and attendant anxieties made the pull of the familiar all the more persuasive. Nothing else out there fit the same way, grooves and notches already filed and moulded. They were too long set in rhythms with which other chords would only jar in raucous dissonance.

Another couple of inches, the smell of red wine and coconut shampoo.

"Can I smoke in here?" he asks the shadow hunched on the bed.

"Yeah."

A hand pushes a switch over the headboard, turning up a few notches on the dimmer switch. The resulting amber light bathes the

109

room in a royal jelly, striking every surface with a velveteen glow. Hilary is propped on one elbow, leaning on a stack of magazines and sipping slowly. Her eyes are closed, pasted together with melted khol.

Lance closes the door behind him. He lights a cigarette, breathes in slowly, savouring the taste melding with her thick air.

"I called you at work. They said you'd been sent home."

"Yeah, that's the nicest way to put it. I'm getting the sack unless I get down on my knees and run my tongue around Jensen's arse-crack. What are you doing here, anyway?"

Her voice is cracking, words spit out like freeze-thawing ice chips. The last is but a courtesy, one of those questions without answers that she prefers, alone, not to ask.

"Hilary…I have some of the red with me. There's enough for us both, but…you remember what she said. About the silence."

Hilary turns this over for a moment. It's easy. It's tempting. It's terrifying.

"I don't know. This is working for me right now." She raises the wine glass, its sloshing contents betraying the climbing tremble in her forearms.

She's lying. Nothing works, now. The rules may have changed, but the board and cup remains the same. These shadows strewing the walls, the open bottle, the music – all a filler, a trailer in the interminable wait. Clean sheets and teeth polished even under the wine stains, toenails shining garnet, tight with polish. All for him. Whether or not he came is beyond the point – the preparations made in the off chance are part of the glue holding her pieces together. There's a clean ashtray on the dressing table, full of the ghosts of the cigarettes she doesn't smoke.

"Hil, I think I'm going out of my mind."

This phrase is the closest he can come to describing the feeling. Taken from pulp novels and gangster movies, it palls in the face of the truth. He's so far entrenched in his mind, in fact, that only the knitting of bone, skin, hair and habit can keep him in the vaguest region of upright. Hilary says nothing. She opens her eyes and stares at him, through him, willing the uncertainty to disappear from view.

He places the cigarette in the ashtray. He leans against the door, pinning Hilary's housecoat beneath the flat of his back. He stares up at the ceiling, palms pressed against his ears, fingers shoved up into his hair, while the cigarette, forgotten, crumbles into a fat ashen caterpillar.

Then he drags his hands from his head, pulling his face downwards into cartoon elongation of itself. He shuffles over to the bed.

"Hil. Say something."

Still, she will not respond. There are too many years of quotes unspoken, pasted to the walls of the skull. As she shakes her head, her hair thrums with light and sound, begging for a touch, but he keeps his arms tightly folded across his chest.

A dog whipped, he whimpers from the nose, drops down on his knees, elbows on a level with the bedspread, but still not touching.

"Hilary. Hilary. This is fucked up. The whole thing. I don't know what I'm doing anymore – not that I ever did, it's just, now...there's nowhere to hide it."

Finally she speaks. Her jaw drops open slowly, as though creaky from disuse. She gulps, her throat full of tannins and tears.

"I can't take this. I mean, I can. I have. I just don't want to."

Whatever she can or cannot take is unclear. Again the having or not, the absence of the actions or their consequence if taken. Their minds dance across the substance and foundation of idioms stretching into eternity. Each pair of eyes trapped in the other, waiting for a green light – or a red one.

Lance drops his hand onto the bed, pressing illusory shapes into the satin, sunbursts or black holes. He drops his gaze.

"Can I...?"

"Not yet. No. No, tell me what you mean to do with the stuff."

Lance withdraws his hand, the tentative point of entry up onto the surface of the bed.

"I mean for us to take it. You heard what Polly said. The more you take, the better it works. The longer it lasts."

Hilary is suddenly in motion, jerking up from her elbows, sitting up straight. She thumps the wineglass on the bedside table as hard as she can without breaking it.

"Yes, Lance, but for *how* long? How many times can we wake up from this? And what the fuck will we have to give her?"

Lance pulls himself tighter, bowing his head to the edge of the bed, and groans, muffled, into the bulk of the duvet. He knows there's only one thing she'll ask for.

He raises his head and inhales deeply, readying himself.

"We have to go back to the theatre and talk to her. She knows we can't afford the money side of it – she'll want something else. More of the same stuff, most likely."

"No. I can't do that again. It's bad enough having it play over and over in my head. I am *not* getting up there again."

"But don't you get it? We felt *nothing* until it was time to leave. We were up there playing a part, nobody has to know any different."

They both know this is untrue – they saw it in the faces of the dispersing crowd. Only theories of relativity kept the scorn from flooding out, the knowledge that, all being there for the same reason, only the passage of time stood between the teller and the tale. The stench of burning flesh was a pretty good indication that the show up on the dais was anything but method acting. Everyone in the room, players and spectators, moved under the prismatic cloud of one or another of Polly's traffic lights.

Hilary sinks back down into the pillow, fingers interlocked across the back of her head, thoughts coasting with the music. Outward, seeping through the curtains, seeking light outside, drifting over the city. To the theatre.

"Lance...?"

"Yeah?"

"What's going to happen to us?"

"I don't know, Hilary. I just don't want to care anymore."

Hilary sits up, swings her feet to the floor and places her hands on his shoulders. A lone tear makes its way down her cheek as her chin shudders, suppressing a sob. His shoulders shake as he, too, begins to weep. This is too much; the usual treatment for tears is out of reach until there's more standing between action and thought.

"Do you have a glass? No? Wait here."

She stands, grateful for a reason to leave the room, still throbbing with indecision. In the kitchen, she takes another goblet from the sideboard. Closing the glass door, she presses her face to it and can't help but be struck by the coolness, still as hard and immovable as it should be, in a sphere where everything is melting like wax. Pulling back, she narrows her eyes at the print left in the pane. She hasn't left, yet, and there are ghosts and warped mirrors everywhere, attesting to her presence, sorely irrefutable. Smearing the image with her empty hand, she turns and walks back to the bedroom, dragging her feet in points behind, as though trying to scrape dog shit from the tips of her toes.

Lance hasn't moved from his kneeling position at the edge of the bed. Hilary pours a glass of wine from the bottle on the dressing table, and hands it to him along with a small pewter coin tray, emptied to accommodate something more precious.

"Sit up. Let's do this."

Lance obeys, moving from the floor to perch on the bed and accepting the glass of wine. He sits edgily, in danger of falling off, still afraid to get too close to something they can't figure out. Not yet. Things must be put in place, first.

He reaches into his coat pocket and removes the red. It's a big one, too, larger than Hilary remembers from last night. Too much confusion in the aftermath of the show, still too high on the last dose, too eager to clothe themselves again and get out of the cramped sauna of the dressing room.

The cellophane whispers as Lance unwraps the package, hissing secrets and promising silence. Tapping the papers on the edge of the tray, he glances at Hilary, searching for the rest of the kit. She hands him a silver straw and one of her business cards, and he cuts two fat lines with his tongue thrust firmly into the side of his mouth. Everything is in place, except the waiting users, still chewing on potential.

"Do you want to go first?" asks Lance.

Hilary nibbles delicately on a lower lip, long since stripped of rouge. This is more than a gamble. The possibility of a clean and empty space inside is ripe, swollen and glossy even as the wrapper crumples. Never has the powder looked so white, so capable of vanquishing stains, erasing contact.

"Are we really going to go through with this?"

"There's no other way," replies Lance, "Unless you can survive the way things are. I know I can't."

He's going blind, losing his way, a moth battering a bare bulb.

"Right. You go first."

Lance returns to his knees, the better for accessing the tray. He places a hand on Hilary's, folded in her lap, and squeezes. First contact in the new awareness of everything: and with the antidote now in place, the last. He leans over, and, eyes still locked upon hers, he takes the hit.

His eyes roll back, as though dropping off to sleep, a beatific smile on his face, accompanied by a sigh of as-yet untapped pleasure. Watching, Hilary no longer has any reservations. She plucks the straw from his hand, and stops her own clocks.

Lance splays out headlong on the floor, watching the ceiling drift off into the gaping firmament. Hilary drops a hand down to grasp one of his, the fingers swirling the air, now tropical with steam generated from benign conflagrations.

Breathing becomes shallow and almost incidental, out of habit as opposed to necessity. The bed and floor beneath bow out from below their bodies, as though suddenly aware of their superfluity. Gravity retreats, to watch and wait, unsure as to whether it will be called upon again. Blue light from the stereo frames its own issue in platinum sparks, as the music rushes in, solidifying where all else dissolves.

This is not a blow as is customary of their history. This is less about damage, than damage control. This is unfelt, a slow filter. Composition fails to exert much claim to the outcome. Instead of the dry whip of the powder, the red drowns, immerses the corporeal in a syrup, the cognitive embalmed, stewed in its own juices and distilled to the purest, unsullied essence of itself. If this could be bottled and sold, there would be no more war, no more hurt or hate or fear. This blurs the line between death and life, awake and asleep, casting aside the strictures surrounding such arbitrary states of being. Most importantly, it rids the hearts and minds of wrong. Whether self-imposed or rained down in sweat and saliva from the baying crowds, there are no longer broken rules. Scourging and castigation are forgotten and brushed off as they are laid down. They now have the night-blindness of the automaton, fragmented into pixels and unaccountable, for as long as the red swims with them through the molasses of the coagulating psyche. It's neither six o'clock nor nine o'clock, midnight nor noon. Time settles in a medicine jar, packed in milk sugar, to be cut and dispensed according to specifications.

The first wave retreats: long enough for Hilary to tug at Lance's hand, a cordial invitation. He sits up, slowly, edging around the eddying spirals of cherry seeping from the walls and across his view. Parting the splashing paint, he locks eyes with Hilary, raising his brows in a question. She nods. He places his arms on the bed, and with effort, pushes himself up onto the bedspread.

They do not fuck, this time. Not from choice, not from the fear that has now gone, effervesced. They do not have to. It is enough, for now, to feel the pressures in familiar places. Lance's head nestled in Hilary's collarbone, his arm across her stomach, his breath fluttering across her chest, her chin resting on the top of his head. Fabric between them grows sticky with sweat and tears. Soon they're swathed in a muggy envelope of wine and last night's insomnia. A kiss takes over, and the room stops moving, each held in suspension with the other in time and space. Pressing lips to lips loses its power, sometimes, amid the thrust for deeper thrills the rooting in chasms. Lips are forgotten, mouths discarded as mere receptacles. The font of all that is said, the channel bearing the elixir of breath, finds its significance realized here, between two lovers on equal planes of want and need. They have here the seam-splitting fulfillment found in drinking deeply, minds and souls merging, a non-invasive osmosis of each into the other.

Even in the absence of dread, hope does not spring. This is escape without marked sanctuary, travel without destination. Self-deception does not ring bells for a better future – for now, it's enough to sink into the holding pattern, the soothing miasma of knowing that things can't get any worse. The pendulum ceases to swing off-course and out of time, settling instead for a leisurely dwindle, rocking them both to a dreamless sleep.

Part XII

Polly has to take Mike for a walk. She's awoken spinning webs of energy around and about her, keen as a knife and hungry for the day's activity to begin. She has much to do, and increasingly short of time as the dates crawl down the calendar.

She makes for the Mike's corner, where he sleeps with bloody murder scrawled across his face.

"Wake up, dear," Polly coos, reaching behind his back to release the cuffs, patting his head as she does so. "Time for a stretch. I'm taking the gag off. No nonsense, okay?"

He nods, grim with the knowledge that there's no-one to hear him even if he did kick up a fuss. Besides, it's not in his best interests to fuck up his end of the deal. More of the same, and everything would be fine. She unties the gag, stuffing it into the pocket of her gown, and leads Mike by the arm to the couch.

"Sit down for a moment."

As he does so, she opens a wooden blanket chest and unearths a neatly folded pile of clothing, tennis shoes perched decorously on top. Presenting these to Mike, she moves to the side of the room and faces the wall, a bizarre gesture implying that he's here of his own free will. A grotesque parody of a morning after a night of misdemeanor: feigning coquetry, allowing him privacy to change.

"I'm ready," he creaks, having scrambled into his clothing, to close contact with her eyes and his skin as quickly as possible. She turns and nods, smiling that knowing smile with which she brings patrons to their knees.

"Come on, then," she beckons.

Mike follows her out of the room, down the stairs. He drinks each dusty breath like mead, simply for its distinction from the air in the chamber, stinking with incense and lunacy, animal droppings and confinement.

At the bottom, at the lobby door, still bolted, he asks,

"When are you going to let me go?"

He isn't expecting much, but there's still enough of his real self in there to wish to draw attention to its itching autonomy. Polly turns predictably nasty, her own special brand, laced with obsequy and emotional blackmail.

"Surely you're not *leaving* me? After everything I've done for you?"

He doesn't reply. It's not a choice – he won't be leaving without her consent, not now or anytime. He knows too much, and before turning him loose, she'll need that knowledge back. Besides, she's not withholding payment. All he need do is what he's told, and the remunerations will be as generous as they have always been. More so. This time he's far beyond the velvet rope – part of her inner circle. She smirks.

"I thought not. We're getting along just fine, don't you think?"

"Yeah. Sure. But...what about Carrie?"

Polly blusters, tired of time-wasting enquiries. What had once seemed a fair enough deal to keep everything looking legit is starting to get on her nerves. Not much longer, now, but Jesus, that girl is a fucking headache.

"Carrie..." she stretches the word as painfully as her jaw will allow, "...is just fine. She sees nothing, she hears nothing, she keeps herself to herself and is usually so tippled by the time she leaves that she wouldn't notice a flock of sheep having a swimsuit parade on their way out the door. Understood?"

Mike lowers his eyes, a chink of remorse opening up under the narcotic clouds. He should have told her what was going on here. But that may have gotten her into real danger. Best that she doesn't know anything, although he's going to miss her.

"Yeah...I guess. I just don't want any of this," he throws his arm up, gesticulating at the staircase leading to Polly's chamber, taking in by default the private theatre, the secrets and lies, the scandals and the transgressions, "to touch her. She's a good kid, but – you know – open to suggestion. She can't have any part in it."

Polly screeches the bolt across the door, swinging it open onto the lobby. Spilling through the glass door, the noon sunshine pushes motes of glittering dust in beams across the hardwood. It's all very clean and quiet, no hints of boot polish or stray peanut shells betraying the activities of the previous evening.

"Look at that," she murmurs, committing it to memory. "How could anything bad ever happen here?"

She grabs Mike by the arm once more, linking it with her own, and proceeds out onto the waiting piazza. In the daytime, the gargoyles and warped caricatures in the awnings and paintings retreat, stripped of their viewing permission by the intercession of the glimmering rays. Their footsteps ring out in wholesome taps, a jaunty stride on a waiting floor. Freedom in incarceration; Mike couldn't have asked for a more congenial prison yard. He wryly twists his mouth. Polly has a way of making things just right. Polished wood and evergreen air freshener; right now it seems adequate enough when held alongside the promise of what waits. A multi-dimensional, all-encompassing breakfast of champions.

"All you have to do, Mike, is behave. And in return, you get everything you could wish for from within my chamber of delights." She whispers lazily, a Disney sorceress.

Mike nods, sleepily. The sudden light and space press down hard, tiring him out with their weight of sensation.

"Shall we go back up?"

He nods again, arm slackening off from its hold in Polly's. They turn about and head back, upstairs, casting dust and doubts aside, back to the font of all that they need.

Polly doesn't bother with the gag, this time. There's no need for it – she's proved, yet again, that even the most despicable of circumstances in which one may find himself remain so only for as long as he is capable of being shocked. Mike hasn't taken as long as she had feared. Now he's quiet, pliant. And line by line he's painted into the family portrait.

Part XIII

They awaken mildly disoriented, but free from drug-sickness. This is not like before. This time there's enough latent energy to prop heads upon necks, enough to fidget life back into numbed feet, enough to keep hands clasped together of their own volition, sweat-glue long since evaporated into the sky. The ceiling is back where it should be; star-gazing had given way to staring at the lengths and colours of each other in the freshness of light afforded by the drug. It's hazy-dark outside, but whether it's dawn or twilight is uncertain. It doesn't matter anyway; they know where to find what they need.

It's working. There's no longer the call for flight that terminates the sense of waking up beside someone open, and opened to. The red has removed the tongue-depressor, the gut-churning, every inch of skin and every filament of hair stretching to the exit.

All feels calm, all seems fine and fair. A great meniscus stretches, a city-sized capsule, a palace of bubble-wrap insulating the cooling flames. The porcelain in the bathroom gleams and chinks, empty of visitors and their customary ablutions. The boiler warms water, needlessly, holding out for a stew of regret. No doors slam, no feet trip on undone laces down the shabby stairs, hightailing for the front door. No, everything is alright.

Lance murmurs into Hilary's hair, pushing against his mouth,

"Morning, I think."

Hilary stretches, catlike, turns and replies,

"Hello…"

Something of a question; she's full of pleasant surprise at the stillness. A stroke along the jawline confirms that this is real, no illusions, no shape-shifting. She leans across him to the bedside cabinet, from which she plucks a tiny digital clock. Green lozenges merely spell out the hour, unfortunately lacking the kick of the others. It's half past nine.

Now comes the gamble. Right now, the breeze is placid enough, ambient temperatures sustained by heat from two bodies in quiet repose. Logic seeks out a chink through which to break, make itself heard. This forethought is unique in its inability to correlate to any sense from an outsider's perspective. It's the junk talking, caressing, slipping threads of contingency into and throughout internal dialogue.

There are two options. It's nothing spectacular – the same catch of the sheets around the feet, the fog of the half-sleep, lies upon any reluctant riser with a duty requiring attention. Circumstances here differ only in the initial prognosis, the voice on the other end of the telephone. No sickness to report, but no insurance against its possible – probable – appearance.

Hilary and Lance undulate in the warm bath of the bedroom air, unwilling to move, but coolly terrified at the prospect of the dream slipping out from the sheath, splitting the seams and leaving them naked and filthy as before.

"We have to…" murmurs Lance.

"I know…" replies Hilary. They remain caught in the same tunnel of thought, each wisp of communication echoing back and forth, unsaid yet understood.

There's plenty of time. Whether or not there's a public performance tonight is beyond the point – half past nine is early doors for the main attraction. What counts is keeping it up, protecting this sensation of salubrious ardor free from the harm inflicted by interference from the real world. A further inoculation is necessary – a trip to Polly's, a deal, a cure, and a bulking of the buffer. At the zenith of pleasure that occupies the slot between fixes, the happy harmony between hit and comedown, they are able just to keep each other warm. When the body builds up a tolerance, however, further means are necessary to ward off the creeping frostbite curling from the toes and fingers, poking at the heart, waiting for an opening.

It only takes a few minutes to unfurl, but seems to last for ages; twin quotation marks coiled around splitting infinitives, they peel slowly. They watch each other dress – no leer of suggestion, but genuine curiosity, having never seen this before in the truth of light. These fumbled, frantic applications of disarrayed attire have always occured under cover of murky dawn, in secret, halfway down the hall and out the front door. Now they watch with indulgence, each dressing the other in affectionate strokes of the eye. Hilary frowns into the mirror of her dresser. She spies yet more imaginary lines, observing them this time with a clinical detachment, strangely unperturbed. Lance stands behind, runs a hand over her shoulder, quelling without words her time-spun anxieties. Tilting her chin up with a curled index finger, he runs the tips of his thumbs along the underside of her eyes, wiping away errant flecks of mascara. Testing to make sure she's real.

She drops her head onto his shoulder, and they embrace tightly, each holding onto the other as though trying to absorb everything held within the other half. Double doors, closing off to everything and everyone else, with the exception of necessary arbitrators between cells and the cosmic plasma they seek. They part with solemnity, readying themselves for a quest for a cup, the mythical elixir with which to dissolve any lingering doubts.

When Evan arrives, bang on seven o'clock, it takes him a few moments to recognize the woman at the ticket stall. He stretches his memory over the contours of her angular face, pencilling khol around the eyes and daubing fluorescent red onto the lips. He replaces her smock cap with a pink Mohawk. Refit complete, he's looking at one of the twins, out of costume and on duty in a more administrative capacity.

"Um...hello..." he chirps, trying hard not to be thrown. He's getting used to it; without being aware of it, the madness in the building has seeped into his bones, leeching off shock by degrees. This is nothing.

"Hi there. Evan, is it?" she replies, in a voice so delicate he's taken aback. Lilting tones from the harsh, wailing revenant of the play are unexpected. She sounds almost childlike, were it not for the cocked brows and purpling around the rims, peeled eggs in a pair of spare tyres.

"Yeah – is Polly around? I'm not sure what I'm supposed to be doing tonight."

The twin nods, casting her eyes down to a ledger upon which nothing is written. Another prop. Smiling sweetly at Evan, she replies,

"Ah, you're back on the bar. You're on by yourself, but you'll be fine – you know there's no show tonight, right? It should be fairly quiet; just the regulars."

Puzzling over the logic of having the bar open without a show crowd to attend to, Evan chalks this up to another of Polly's quirks. He supposes it *is* a nice enough bar in which to pass the time, classier than most of the joints on the rest of the strip. He's less enthused about manning it by himself – despite being better versed now in the ways and workings, he suspects that without Carrie nearby as an amulet, he'll lose the rhythms he gained in her presence.

"Sure…Joe not around?"

"Nope, it's his week off. That's why I'm on foyer duty myself. We're all part of the team in this place – without many traveling revues to break it up, even the performers become staff members if need be."

Evan can imagine. The switching of roles in and around the place is fluid to the point of being almost creepy – nobody seems to have a fixed position, except perhaps Polly herself. Keeping the bar open suddenly makes more sense, especially in light of Joe's earlier comments about the skewing of the books. He's yet to see much cash changing hands for anything other than drinks, and even at that, so many favors are called and liberties taken as to cast doubts on how the place ever made any money. He chuckles, replies,

"I've noticed, folks in here seem pretty capable of all the jobs in the place. Just so long as we amateurs aren't expected to tread the boards…!"

The twin sparkles from incisors to molars, exposing each of her platinum fillings in turn in a wicked grin. She knows better than to hint at the arbitrary relevance of labeling spectator and spectacle, not here, and not while he's clearly still fresh. She settles instead with the basics.

"Well, you know where everything is. I'm sure Polly will swing by at some point, just to check in with how you're getting along. According to the customers, you're doing a marvelous job."

Evan smiles shyly, unremarkably susceptible to flattery in his relative youth.

He makes for the bar, simultaneously admonishing and praising himself for having avoided asking after Carrie. She doesn't work here, after all. She made it perfectly clear last night that she comes and goes as and when she pleases. Still, there was that step for a hint…something about catching up soon? Borrowing his mother's savoir faire, he resolves to treat any reappearance as a gift, not a given. Besides, he's pretty sure that even with just the regulars this evening, he'll have plenty to keep him occupied. Even if his mind still played over spinning batons, shuddered over amber eyes.

Part XIV

Carrie wakes with a mouthful of damp cotton. She'd fallen asleep across her mother's lap, each lulling the other into an embrace of exhausted fury. Spitting fibres from between her teeth, she sits up and shakes the imaginary rubble from her hair.

Tracy stirs, stomach growling, trembling slightly along each arm. Her knees begin to shiver in jig, shifting Carrie further onto her own portion of the couch.

"I'm sorry, hen…I must have needed that."

"No, mum. Think we both did."

Tracy yawns widely, pushing words from around the vacuum.

"I remember when I was wee, whenever I was in a rager about something: your gran would always send me to my room and tell me to have a bit of a cry. She said it does the world of good to clean the pipes, let some of the pressure off the brain."

Tracy relies a great deal on inherited gems of wisdom from her elders. It used to irritate her how well the tips worked, particularly when issuing from the infrequent target of her angers. Household witches with their clever disguises never cease to be relevant even now – simple solutions to simple problems, gallingly incongruent to the skepticism picked up with age and experience. She throws up a prayer of thanks every now and again, just in case. Carrie is coming round to the idea, although she has less investment in the power of a sobbing session to expurgate the desire for vengeance.

"I see what she means, kind of. Listen, I still can't figure out who put that *stuff* on our doorstep, but when I do - "

"Never mind about it, hen. It's done and by with. I'm not that bothered anymore what folk think of me, I just don't want you to get hurt yourself."

This is a futile prospect in the tightened spheres of association in a conurbation with such stock in family ties. Whether passed up or down a generation, shame and scandal thrive in the niches between genes.

"Don't worry about me. I can handle myself."

Tracy grabs Carrie around the shoulders in a violent hug, squeezing tightly to the grit she knows nestle there, shards of Frank, pressing through the skin.

"I know you can. I'm so proud of you, okay? I know I don't say it often, or much of anything like that at all, but I am. So many girls your age are away out misbehaving and causing havoc, dropping out of school and getting pregnant too young. I hear all about it in the hairdressers. You're not like that. You're too clever. Sometimes I wonder where you got it from."

Carrie hugs back, delicately, feeling slightly invaded. Waking up with her face in her mother's armpit was bad enough, but this was pushing it somewhat. Slowly she disentangles herself, leans back and lowers her eyes. She doesn't quite want to hint that Tracy's been a greater influence than she knows – primarily in the respect that Carrie wants nothing of what she has, to be nothing like what she is, and angles her desired trajectory firmly in the opposite direction.

"I dunno, mum. We get by, though, huh?"

She means it, too. She and Tracy have their moments in battle, but, bearing in mind socio-economic lessons carried down from the same household goddesses as before, and from adverse examples screamed out in hairdressers and on public transportation, their domestic arrangements are healthier than many she can call to mind. Bills paid, sometimes on time; plumbing and heating mostly in working order; enough spare cash to supplement the wine in the fridge with the occasional pint of milk and loaf of bread – things could be much worse. Walls remain perpendicular to the floor and roof; a decent place to start when tabulating the material ways of things.

Tracy twists one corner of her mouth in wry agreement. There's something to be said for the peace and quiet; Carrie's lack of interference with her affairs and space allowed her to go about her business in relative privacy. She sometimes takes a lover, someone with whom to pass the playing fields of time between work and sleep, Friday night and Monday morning, but she regards these men as optional extras, as opposed to necessities.

"I suppose so. You and me against the world, eh?"

"What about Kevin? Thought you guys were getting pretty cozy."

Kevin hasn't called since the other night. His ardor has evidently cooled somewhat, possibly on the back of Tracy's ever-more apparent financial decrepitude.

"He's not a part of this family, and he never will be. He's a nice fella, but he's still too wet behind the ears. Plus, he was getting a bit too comfy in here for his own good, ay? Lassies like us need our space."

This is the first time that Tracy's ever drawn attention to her penchant for younger men, never mind her dawning recognition that such guys carry flaws alongside their birth-dates. Maybe it's a consequence of Carrie's approaching birthday; that Tracy can now talk freely about matters of the heart, woman to woman. Or perhaps it's a sign that Tracy herself is growing up, still learning – Carrie's struck that, even with age in their favor, adults don't know everything about the ways of the world.

"Nothing you couldn't handle, mum. Is he coming over? More to the point; are you going to be alright?"

Tracy nods, smiles. She'll be fine as soon as she gets a window opened onto some undisturbed drinking time, whether or not Kevin decides to show. Clearly, Carrie plans to be out again tonight. Tracy briefly wonders who she's spending all of her time with – she never brings friends home, never really mentions names unless pushed, probably because so many were tied up with the theatre.

"I'll be fine. Don't know about Kevin – think he's working. You going out?"

Carrie grimaces, unsure of appropriate protocol, conscious that she's in danger of selfishness. Tracy's lying – she has no idea what Kevin's up to, and she knows Carrie knows. There is that hunger in Tracy's expression though, that yen for the conversion of weak tea to cheap gin, a situation whose comfort relies upon the absence of an impressionable teenage daughter. They're each dancing around half-hearted requests, unsure solicitations, when both really want the same thing: peace to do their own thing, unmolested by disapproval or disappointment.

"Not if you don't want me to," replies Carrie, gritting her teeth.

"Of course I do, love. I'd much rather you were out having fun than stuck in here. You still hanging out with that fella...what's his name again, Mick?"

"Mike. And yeah, I see him every now and then."

"Not a boyfriend then?" Tracy's anxious to crank the conversation down from the high-gravity subject matter still afloat. Teen romance did the trick, every time. Plus, knowing how little information Carrie typically gives away, the conversation would be over that much quicker, hastening the move toward re-equilibrium. Despite the rarity of their heart-to hearts, mother and daughter manage to maintain a conversational poise that keeps them both quite satisfied, each getting what they want without too much argument.

"Nah. Just a mate."

"Ach well, it's better to keep them that way, I reckon. Wouldnae give up on men altogether, but at least when you're just pals you can both just come and go as you please, no strings."

Carrie avoids pointing out the obvious – that Tracy's men were, by and large, commitment-phobic charlatans with absolutely zero conception of what it might mean to be a 'boyfriend', its attached fidelity as pliable as the label itself. Certainly the only strings attached were the ones rooted in Tracy's hands and head, not to mention her fridge door and purse. However, it was all the more reason to get the hell out as soon as possible. The nursery story about the Emperor's new clothes crosses her mind - she can't remember how it ended, but she doesn't imagine the main man was terribly forgiving of his humiliation at the hands of the leering crowd, or whether he believed his rioting subjects at all. Tracy probably knows already that she sits on a throne of bottled grief, but it'll be of her own reckoning to eventually see the truth, no longer blinded by the glint of broken glass. She'll have to throw down her own spectacles to see jeweled citadels for what they really are – illusions, mainly self-perpetuated, and impenetrable as yet to the ugly truths of art-student high-school journal-keepers.

"Aye, you're right. I don't have time for the boyfriend shite anyway; I've got art projects and stuff on the go. Plus the occasional shift. Which is where I'm off to tonight – new kid on the rota, needs some help to keep the peace."

Tracy's less bothered than usual about the site of Carrie's extra-curricular activities. It's so far removed from the house, the neighbourhood, the community ill-feeling. She remembers the vague glimmer of magic to be had, back in the days with Frank, when everything was on an even keel. Back when she thought all that stuff was pretty cool, instead of a drain on finances, time, companionship and love. She can't begrudge Carrie the same magpie predispositions she once had herself.

"Well, you know that place better than anyone. I'm sure you'll have everything in hand. Erm...do you need money, or anything? Dinner? I could ring you a takeaway."

Maintaining the role of efficient and concerned parent, Tracy pays more attention than she gives herself credit for, but tends to break out her weaponry at the most inopportune and awkward moments. She's skint, for a start, and ordering greasy slop the quasi-Chinese joint will just prolong contact when all she wants to do is get back to some serious floating.

Even the closest of families are not built for prolonged and unlimited contact. So many disparate beings of different ages shouldn't be expected to share everything. Space is precious; free and priceless, and crucial for each entity to maintain their individual traits – not to mention habits.

Carrie still has change left over from the previous evening. She'll manage. She just needs some air, away from the gloom and banality suffocating the house.

"Nah, I'm fine. Sure you'll be okay?"

"Aye."

Carrie gives her mother an awkward hug, before bolting upstairs to ready herself for another night out. Only when she's rummaging in her drawers and closet does it strike her that Tracy's omitted to ask about school. Carrie hadn't bothered going, not even for the afternoon, since she got her last bollocking.

The first bus to arrive is a double-decker. Carrie has loved them since her childhood. There is still something irrationally exciting about sitting in the front seat on the top deck of such a huge machine – like flying, almost, all the city rushing in toward her. Tree branches wallop the front window like protesting natives, warding off the intrusion of the massive metal behemoth.

She sinks back into the seat, allowing the darkening sunlight to wash over in apricot blossom, unhindered by the squat pre-fabrications which delineate the route into the city. Golden balm slowly makes way for sharp pricks of light in the high-rises, then the tentative flickers of neon as the main drags prepare for the coming evening.

Approaching the hub, the older buildings fill the window, their towers and niches throbbing with the dying light. Glasgow really is beautiful when one knows where to look. She can picture old world gargoyles and filigree-clad angels conversing over the heads of the passing crowd. This is it, the flight, the escape not from reality, but from one stream of desperation to another. The top deck may make the beauty of the architecture much more accessible, but she can't fly forever on the whims of a clear day. The pavement isn't as far away as it seems, still streaked with chaos. Sometimes, graffiti makes it up even to this height, courtesy of certain bloody-minded appetites for destruction. A seraphim perched on a marble dais has two acrid-yellow nipples spray-painted across her chest. She looks up and far away, refusing to acknowledge the desecration. Carrie follows her gaze, sighing, waiting for the right moment to descend the steps. She has to time it just right, preferably at a reliably slow set of traffic lights, in order to keep her balance on her way down. All too often she loses her footing at a sudden acceleration, grappling the handrail and strafing her arms with friction burns.

Her stop approaches. She makes it out and down onto the concrete without accident. Trongate thrums like a hive, as late shoppers clash with early pub-goers, each contingent thrusting members of the opposition out onto the road to reach their destinations. Pile-ups of buses converge in the streets, most passing stops without bothering to stop – kinder drivers will open the doors when paused at red lights, allowing more athletic travelers to board. You had to be quick, alert and mobile around this time of day – no allowances are made for walking-sticks, heavy shopping, paraplegia or myopic squinting at the numbers on the front of the vehicle.

Carrie slips as delicately as she can between the irate and the ignored, enjoying the free space to make her destination in her own time. It's a rare thing to move around the city without an agenda, something she appreciates only in the eye of the cyclone of carnage. The tramps have been blocked from doorways by the closed partitions, and receive much abuse from passing drunkards. She chucks a handful of change into a torn paper cup, frustrated but powerless, chalking it up to yet more experience on that blackboard of truths so at odds with her youth. Breaking through the crowds and across the road, the glorified boulevard of Argyle Street affords the chance of a breath, a movement without contact. She's herself again, flowing out of the amorphous mass of the multitudes.

It's the wrong kind of open space. Plenty of room to move around, but too many people, still, too much noise pressing in from all sides. Like being trapped between bars of rolling static on a TV without signal, riding radio waves playing gibberish. Round the corner, second left, there's an alley, running down the back doors of the bars and takeaways framing the strip. Less of a shortcut, more like an alternate route, off the beaten track and free from casual tourists. Carrie slides her hands from her pockets, placing one on the strap of her bag, and steps into a pace that's determined without being hurried. She's never gotten much trouble before, aside from the occasional flasher or disoriented smackhead, but it doesn't hurt to be ready to fly, in the off chance the city throws up a more violent breed of nutcase.

A cluster of waiters, from the Tuscan restaurant out front, perch on the rims of empty beer kegs and smoke roll-up cigarettes. A flurry of mixed dialect bounces off the alley walls, as the Glaswegian staff curse like Mafioso whilst the Italians drop consonants into the ether. They nod at Carrie as she passes, she tilts her head in response. Further up, a landfill of empty beer crates and fruit cartons marks territories between the pub and smoothie bar. The mass emits a groan, then the snick of a flint strike. She climbs over and around the debris. A vagrant in torn canvas overalls reclines against a wheelie bin, igniting a cigarette from a lighter held by a youngish bartender. From the front of a capacious pinafore, the barman extracts a tinfoil package, handing it to the battered splinter. He flashes a mouthful of varicolored teeth in reply. Carrie nods again, walks past, turning her head for a second look. The homeless guy unwraps a sandwich, nothing pharmaceutical, but certainly a medicine of sorts. Carrie grins widely, inexplicably pleased to have witnessed this private exchange. It would be a moment of restored faith in humanity, an epiphany of sorts, if she were a sucker for that kind of thing. Still, little glimmers help to knock chinks in the strangling shell of malevolence that envelops the city. She presses on, racing the sunset, in time to watch night fall entirely from the window of the bar.

Twin Number Two – at least, she's almost positive, going just by the voice – is on the podium, greeting a slow wave of customers. Carrie pauses.

"Hey. Joe not in?"

Twin lowers her eyelids from tilted-doll height, relaxing in the presence of an almost-equal.

"Nah, holidays due, apparently. The new guy's in, though. Seems nice enough."

"Mike's still not in either?"

Twin drops her lids even further, into a precarious scowl. Questions are not part of her remit; interrogations even less so.

"I don't think he'll be back. You'd have to ask Polly for sure, but, last I heard, he's moved onto something...more stimulating, I think he said."

Carrie's less surprised by the news than she'd expect. Mike was a good mate, in a big-brother kind of way, but he'd been a bit off lately. Reflecting on their last few conversations, he'd seemed more noticeably stoned than usual, and much less keen to have her around. Whenever he did say more than a few words at a time, he complained about the job, the people, always citing madness at the theatre without ever running into detail. Still, he hadn't said goodbye.

"No...messages   or   anything?   No   leaving   party?" Twin shakes her head, suppressing the urge to tell the little upstart to shut up and move it along.

"No. Nothing. Like I say, you'd have to ask Polly."

"Oh. Right. Well, I'm gonna go and check on Evan – told him I'd swing by and give him a hand, if he needs it."

Part XV

Evan isn't doing too badly. The place fills at a steady, manageable rate; folks drifting in pairs or quartets, selecting simple drinks from the tips of tongues, regular as clockwork. He begins to acquire a rhythm, picking up expectations from fleeting glimpses as the customers approach. Two older women: ice, three cubes, wedge of lime, splash of gin, then fizzing tonic from the mixer gun oscillating between glasses. A gentleman with a younger female on the arm; flick a wine glass from the gantry, stem clutched between forefingers, chink an iced pint glass against the lager tap, press and hold with one hand, pour the wine with the other. Four blondes, nipped into suits and pointed shoes, means ice bucket, sparkle, corks flying, four champagne flutes. Easy.

Carrie watches through the porthole in the door, more than a little piqued by the surge of interest fluttering in her gut. It's probably guilt – she knows she's here for chat and escape, instead of staying home with Tracy. There's only one reliable cure to take the edge off, knowledge gleaned first through observation, then through experience. a smattering of ethanol: tinkling against the inside of the skull, settling the clamour in the gut.

She opens the door and enters, unable at first to catch Evan's eye. He's following her example from the night before – holding glasses up to the light, polishing with a linen napkin, checking carefully for smudges. Ignoring the booths, the quiet huddles, she strides to the bar and propels herself up into a bar stool, placing an elbow on the counter and waiting for him to turn.

When he does so, his face breaks into a wide grin for a moment, before he reins it in, settling for a cool but welcoming spread.

"Hi," he begins.

"Hello…I came by to give you a hand, but it looks like you've got it covered!"

She's pleased to see it all working so well – even at seventeen, there's satisfaction to be taken from watching an imparted lesson bearing out so satisfactorily. Her actions and advice coming together to produce an agreeable synchrony. There's still that tiny tingle of disappointment, though, that superfluity awards even the most charitable guru. Another uncomfortable spasm best addressed with a beverage.

"Aye, it's been quiet, though – I mean, none of that rush from last night. Can you believe Polly's not been by? I'm still doing that Mike guy's job, not sure if I'm supposed to. I don't think she even knows *who* does *what* in this place."

Carrie nods.

"Yeah, as you'll have noticed, Polly favors the all-hands on-deck approach. Jobs and staff in here are always a bit confused. Folk have either worked here for what seems like forever, or they high-tail it without a second's warning. You like it enough here to want to stay?"

Hearing the latter streaming direct from the Desperation Alcove at the rear of her consciousness, she's kicking herself. Evidently she's more burned than she realized by Mike's disappearance without a word of goodbye. Evan doesn't detect anything untoward – too busy drinking in the fluids of her hair and skin to clock the increase in pitch. She's still too much of a sensory explosion to take in all at once.

"Yeah, it's a pretty cool job, all things considered. I used to work in a grocers' – this definitely beats ripping boxes for a living."

She laughs, tinkles undercut with just the right amount of acerbic irony.

"I suppose every job has its drawbacks. Hopefully you'll escape some shite working in here – at least there's a bar between you and the punters, and making drinks keeps you busy instead of having to sit still all night, watching the same stupid play over and over again."

"Oh, fuck, I'm sorry – listen to me blathering away here. Would you like a drink?"

She hadn't meant it as a dropped hint, but now that he mentions it, she did have some quality self-medicating to get into gear.

"Sure, if you're not too busy. Think I'll start with something different tonight…"

She peruses the gantry, paying no attention, simply drawing out the time between utterances to slacken the odds of saying something stupid. Her eyes alight on a dark brown bottle, rounded like a genie's lamp, hinting at an inclination if not quite promising three wishes.

"I'll have a Drambuie, please. Just ice."

Evan obliges, taking time to select and polish a brandy balloon. He's learning to take it easy on the strictures, too – free-pouring a decent slosh of tawny nectar over the ice, no measures, all instinct: the confident hand of a chef gilding a delicacy, an arms expert unpeeling a bomb.

"Thanks. Nicely done."

Her cheeky wink implies an understanding of the contentment achieved by the simplest of tasks. He eyes the comps book for a second, wondering whether Carrie's drinks would affect the stock measures any more than the crazy whims of most of the crowd. He passes, figuring he'd explain later if need be.

"No worries. So…why Drambuie tonight? Most folks seem to have a favourite, a habit. You don't seem to have a drink of choice – do you?"

She rolls a mouthful around her tongue, again stacking odds against unleashing a stream of idiocy.

"Not really. I know what I like, but I mix it up whenever I can. Heard someone say, once, that if you stick to the same thing you're more likely to develop a habit – apparently it's not how much you drink, but how much of the same thing, that makes you an alcoholic. It's a load of crap, of course, but there's no harm in keeping it in mind…just to make sure."

This is fine. This little nugget of wisdom could have come from any idle gossip or tatty magazine; nobody but Carrie needs to know that it was the topic sentence of an argument between her parents. Evan cocks a brow, curious. He chalks it up to something he'd rather learn by proxy.

"Makes a bit of sense, I guess – it's probably harder to keep track of how much you're drinking if it's the same taste in your mouth all the time."

Conversation ceases; Carrie can't think of anything to say that will guide it beyond the over-familiar subject of excessive drinking – especially when she's trying to enjoy her liqueur. Evan does her a favor.

"So…what do you do when it's this quiet? There's plenty of folk in, but none of them want anything yet."

"I watch them, I guess. The people you get in here are often pretty good sources of entertainment, even when they're behaving themselves. Sometimes they'll talk to you, but only when they're a bit greased already."

Evan glances around the bar, searching for speckles of interest. Much of it sits in perusing eccentric attire, calculating the value of garments, much of which sits in inverse proportion to their questionable chic. In a corner booth, an aging cardsharp sprays a handful of playing cards over a trio of businesswomen, apparently having botched a trick. Evan keeps his gaze level, watching, waiting. The man reaches under the shirt collar of one of the women and extracts a Jack of Clubs, to a squeal of amazement from the table. He's not as out of practice as he'd appeared at the first glimpse, an observation reinforced by the unexpected production of a posy of freesias from the hatband of his trilby. He presents it to the woman with a flourish, then the table simmers down into its own magic trick – glasses of wine sliding down eager throats in a great and unrivalled disappearing act.

"Everyone in here has a story to tell, or a secret to keep," remarks Carrie, following his gaze. "That guy was kicked out of the Magic Circle for trying to poison a fellow magician. Some sort of dispute over copyrighting a trick."

"Jesus, you kidding me? He was so...*upright* when he was up at the bar – asking everyone what they wanted, insisting he paid..."

"As corny as it may sound, nothing's ever what it seems in a place like this. You'd think the illusions would be confined to the stage, but they're not. Nothing stays the same for long enough to put a finger on what it is that's so *weird* about this joint – probably for the best, you'd go mad trying to puzzle it out."

As if to further back her up, an experiment in time travel barrels through the door. Hilary and Lance look both ten years older and ten years younger, all at the same time. They've clearly been at it pretty hard with whichever poison of choice they'd elected to carry them through the few days since she's last seen them. Hilary looks embalmed; tired, shrunken flesh weeps from clenched bones and rustles within a suit that's suddenly too large, flapping around wishbone femurs. Lance looks exhumed after a premature burial – waxen skin scored with dark bruises pressed into his cheeks and around his eyes, coffee-colored hair so incidental in that pale skin it looks grafted on.

134

Yet, they move with a youthful languor and ease, arms linked in mirth, faces turned up toward each other. When they take a seat at the bar, both Evan and Carrie are stunned by the brilliance of their eyes – twin-sets of bottle green and cerulean, set in a white so pure as to seem almost violet, color impervious to the surrounding red of the lids. Child's eyes, newborn, absorbed and astonished in their waking dreams.

In synch, Carrie and Evan turn their heads quickly from the newcomers, so as not to be caught staring. Not in those orbs.

Part XVI

"I don't know what I want. I've forgotten what I like, Lance."

"Should we ask what they think?"

Lance directs an eyebrow at the lanky guy in the black shirt, standing behind the bar. He's deep in conversation with a girl in jeans and a fringed suede jacket, leaning across the counter over a glass of something amber. Hilary ferrets around in her catalogue of conventions, dredging to the surface some manner of being in this alien, yet familiar, room.

"If you get a pint, I'll have what she's having. It looks pretty."

Lance runs the words around his mouth, practicing, before catching Evan's eye. Placing a top hat and tails upon his utterances, squinting through an imaginary monocle, he manages to wring out his request.

"Evening…a pint of…Guinness? Please? And a glass of…" he points at Carrie's drink. "Whatever the young lady's having, for my companion, please."

He slumps back as far as the bar stool will allow, exhausted by the outpouring of relative sense. Evan rattles up the drinks, trying, like Carrie, not to listen. Or look like he's listening. They're talking nonsense, words copied and pasted from annals of popular memory and dregs of advertising campaigns.

"This is lovely. It tastes pretty, too," murmurs Hilary, nonsensically, upon tasting her drink. "If only the other stuff tasted like this."

"I suppose it's like Polly says – it's what you make of it."

"I wish she'd get a move on. I'm still hearing colours, but I can't smell sounds anymore. Need a top-up before…"

"Before it's all back to normal, yeah?"

"Normal. Can't bear it. Hard enough being around so much of it...oh...hold it..."

Something else draws fingernails across the surface of Hilary's perception. Payment. She rummages in her purse, inciting Lance to reach for his wallet also. Evan has forgotten entirely to ask for a sum, too baffled by the couple and less than eager to meet their eyes again. A drift of coins appear on the bar, at which Hilary stares, comprehending nothing. She places a fingertip on a two-pound coin, the largest in the pile, and pushes it around the counter, unsure what it means.

"This one?" she asks, as a foreigner might, before bursting out in a giggle. "I don't know what they're for, anymore!"

Evan curbs the urge to shake his head in disbelief, tuning into his memories of his mum's dealings on holidays in the Algarve.

"Em...no. These ones, see?" Evan slowly counts out the correct payment. "One, two, three, four, five pounds and ten, twenty, thirty, fifty pence. Yeah?"

Hilary's giggling fit passes over to Lance, who buckles in two over the bar, pushing the rest of the coinage in the wake of the exact sum. "Keep it, keep it, friend, we're just here to kill some time anyway," he chuckles. He presses his forehead to Hilary's, and they quiver with mirth, as though sharing some private joke by osmosis, passed from skin to skin.

It seems indecent to invade a moment of such privacy: Evan moves further down the bar, back toward Carrie, praying for a sudden surge of activity from the rest of the punters. Carrie raises an eyebrow, more than accustomed to the madness, but amused nonetheless by Evan's reaction.

"See what I mean?" she mutters, "They're all off their fucking nuts in here."

Around the corners of his mouth, Evan asks,

"What comes first, then? The nutters or the theatre? They can't all be mad, unless there's some sort of advert on the Internet or something."

He doesn't need to keep his voice down: they're too immersed in each other to pay the slightest modicum of attention to anything outside of their own three square feet.

Carrie can't be sure anymore, it was like trying to find the edge of the Sellotape. Fumbling and picking away at what was, and what seemed – too much of a hardship, easier just to float along the top.

"My gran used to say that people came here to escape: from boredom, from poverty, from their real lives. I guess it's not too much of a stretch to see people coming to escape from their own heads. Play around in the weirdness with like-minded folk."

She doesn't add that Polly definitely has a hand in this upsurge – the punters definitely bring some otherworldliness with them, and it can't all burst out of a vacuum.

One of the mimes strolls into the bar, this time in traditional black and white. Right in the concentric circles of his gaze, he fixes the summoned clients. Nobody notices, or seems to care, that a monochrome clown stalks the ground outside of the auditorium. Evan sighs, possibly weary of theatrical flourishes when he's just trying to get the job done. The mime places a hand on the shoulders of each of the pair, spinning them around in their stools. He says nothing, as is customary of his profession, but points to the door, then upwards. Mutely, they rise, trailing the silent messenger to the hub of the organism.

Part XVII

Polly ponders lighting a few more candles, and decides against it on the basis that everything will be bright enough in time. She's dressed for illumination tonight – a hoary canvas smock over matching trousers. The tunic fastens with winking steel toggles, oddly sharp at the tip, like a string of bullets or long canines cast in pewter. Mike is back in the corner, although this time she's left him free of cuffs and gag. He's sleeping, tired after his walk and spinning through his dose. She's given him an ottoman upon which to sit – he's been on his best behavior, and she keeps her promises when it comes to rewards.

Christian shouldn't be too much longer. She'd thought about going to fetch Lance and Hilary herself, but the though of fending off enquiries on all sides from other, less involved, clients, made her head ache with impatience. Besides, Christian had been hankering after something to do – like the rest of the cast, he hates quiet nights. Having to wait for after-hours for any action makes him feel naked; even in full make-up, his skin was itchy and useless without the glances of the crowd to buoy him along.

The animals are more restless than usual – the birds shift around in the cage, the rabbit scampers across the floor, ticking claws along the wood. She scoops the rabbit up into her arms, then places it in Mike's lap, tousling his hair.

"Mike! Wake up. I need you to take care of Boris for a spell – he's a touch overexcited, what with our guests arriving."

Mike grunts, shaking sleep from his eyes. He stares down at the crop of white fur, bemused, before Polly's words filter through. He gifts her with a dopey smile, before burrowing his face into the back of the animal, wrapping the twitching mass in his arms and dropping back into sleep. Polly shrugs, and drapes a fleece blanket over the bird cage. The door-knocker rattles from the outside. They're here.

Hilary couldn't let go of Lance's hand even if she wanted to. He grips back tightly, the ferocity indicative of the slow tumble of the red from his system.

Hairs are beginning to stand on end as successive washes of heat and cold swell over limbs and torso, tightening and slackening. It's not unbearable yet, but unless it's addressed quickly, nothing will suffice but to clamber from the skin, clawing and shaking.

"Come in."

Polly speaks in a measured tone reserved for these final rulings, bolstered by the omission of her standard pleasantries and redundant reiterations. She has turned off the pomp and bombast, making it clear that this penultimate session must not be taken lightly. She has patted herself down for any fripperies, zoning into the core of her vernacular and mannerisms. This is not a performance – they're beyond needing convinced. By the set of their jaws, eyes bristling out over sockets, they're here for the real deal.

They don't wait to be asked to sit down – they do so feverishly, keen to take a seat before they collapse. Still they cling to each other, anchors weathering the incoming tempest. Matching eye to eye, grip for grip, desperation for desperation, they shiver and perspire, staring up at the directress. A rustle from Mike's corner sends them both into a spasm of panic. Hilary turns, sees the man and the rodent, and blurts,

"Who's he? You promised you'd see us before anyone else!"

"Calm down. He's not a customer, he's an employee. I'm training him up in the finer ends of the business."

Lance follows Hilary's look, and a glimmer of familiarity breaks the surface on the alarm. He recognizes the man in the corner from somewhere, not long ago, either.

"Isn't that…" he murmurs.

"Yes. He tired of the bar work, and sought a promotion. He has a better deal, now. But that's of no matter. You're here to seal the deal."

It is not a question. Inside each of her customers is a trigger, an overflow, a level to which they might play around before reaching a point from which there is no turning back. Hilary and Lance have been in it all the way from the first time. Self-deluding and protests to the contrary notwithstanding, Polly has been sitting on a pair of exceptionally loyal and pliable customers since the night they first entered her chamber. Before, even. She knows more about them than they know of themselves – she's seen it raw and bloodied, whipped

140

and broken, cross-sectioned and displayed under slides and spotlights. This is what they've been seeking for a long time.

Lance takes the platform, still unsure about the moulding of words around his mouth, but edgy enough to hustle the proceedings along, to close the gaps before they collapse into chasms, unable to be scrambled from again.

"We want everything you can give us. We have to keep this…this…whatever it is, we can't go back now to the way things were."

Polly sits down on the opposite sofa. She crosses her ankles primly, placing her hands on her knees, drawing up every fibre of gravity into her posture.

"I think I have been very honest with you throughout our dealings. I have not misled, misrepresented or overcharged. I have exacted payment in direct correlation to the goods I have given, and within the parameters of that which was discussed prior to their assignation. Am I correct?"

They nod, barely understanding a word, carried along by the awareness that she seeks an affirmative answer.

"I shall remind you of the consequences I mentioned before. The product I have given you does not suffer from the diminishing returns that plague much of the others on the market. Not only is each dose as effective as the last – it is more so. The results are stronger and longer-lasting each time. This is therefore a drug to be taken for the long-term – there is no detox, no clean time, no wagon-jumping. Do you understand?"

Again they nod, more frenetically, skin cells jolting as if through a grater.

"We understand," Hilary clamors, "We do. We'll do anything, now. We can't give this up even if we wanted to. It's too awful."

Polly lowers her eyebrows. This is too easy. They're both still terribly young, they must have some fight left.

"What's so awful that you'd rather disappear? Have you no imagination?"

She doesn't mean it, of course, she knows that there's nothing out there as powerful as the contents of her wooden box. The war with the self takes place on more levels than she can count, these days. So many of the faceless, the hopeless, the empty, self-medicating any way they can justify within the realms of the socially acceptable. Shopping, gambling, spa weekends, organized and disorganized religion, new shoes, manicures, spray tanning, rhinoplasty...so many options, so little effect. There is the potential for laughter, here – Hilary and Lance have both tried everything at least once. Polly knows better. Here we have the theatre, the stage, the spotlight, the connections, then the reverse – the disconnections, the hiding, the silence, the darkness. Watching and being watched – validation, freedom, plucking fragments from the players with which to patch the self, wrestling out of the flesh cage on stage, snakes in a barrel, flaying each other in desperation to shed their own skin.

Lance is blank, yet summons the words as if from some internal script machine.

"Imagination is killing us both. We need to get away. It's been too long, we've gotten too sick, and we need a cure. You have one."

Polly leans forward, nodding slowly, then stopping with an abrupt jerk of the head.

"What's a cure with no future? I can't explain it more clearly than this: I can give you what you want, but the solution works only inside. Nothing on the outside will change – you will simply be inured to the sensations. You won't be of the world, but moving along the surface. Can you cope with that?"

Polly is trying very hard to manage her words, imparting only what is necessary, withholding an outpouring, slinging adverbs and qualifiers over one shoulder. This interrogation remains pointless – whether or not the current state of play is manageable or reparable, it still palls in comparison to the offer of silence.

She hasn't offered a complimentary touch-up just yet. She's allowing the old sensation to creep back in, just enough to remind her customers of the alternative to the proposition. She needn't have bothered. But it didn't do to make assumptions.

To the practicalities, then. Polly watches them slide down the back of the sofa, puddles of withdrawal, submissive now as they ever will be.

"Now, I am aware that you both have jobs and homes of your own. Do you have family?"

She tacks the latter on in full knowledge of its absurdity, given the twisted ties between the two.

"No. Our father died a few years ago. It's just Lance and me left."

Hilary's voice wavers, keen to move on. Polly doesn't linger over the ghost; she can make her own guesses as to how the father ceased to be.

"Jobs, then. You are not under any obligation to remain here indefinitely, however: you do have your responsibilities to fulfill, and moonlighting becomes a strain rather early on in each of my clients. I would therefore advise that you give your notice as soon as possible."

"What about..."

She cuts Lance dead.

"You're worried about bills, mortgages and the like, I see. Can you think of a single thing you want to purchase outside of these unfortunate necessities? Anything your wages can buy that will bring you any kind of satisfaction?"

She waits for marquees of luxury items to pass before eyes. Shoes, bags, keys to expensive cars, lipsticks, pewter candy dishes, silver straws and spoons, all drifting past on a rippling tide of silk. Now the symbols of being in a sphere of clout are out of context and out of time. Around these items, a glistening net is cast, dragging them back into the ways of before. Sacrifices must be made, and handing over the goods is no longer the hardship it may once have been. These mean nothing more than slipping off the veils, going back to the desolate landscapes in which they were just ornaments, dried roses in a cracked vase, polythene sheets over a corpse. Technicalities, showing off more decay than they hide.

Hilary and Lance can't deal in numbers and gloss anymore, it's all pointless.

"You can have everything." Lance makes a move for his wallet, then places hands back into Hilary's at the shaking of Polly's head.

"I don't want anything except your work, your loyalties. The question is simply whether there's anything holding you back from giving yourselves over fully to what will be a new way of things."

It's taken long enough. Too long, dredging for clues, seeking buried treasure. They're here for the final straw. They're twitching, scratching, coiled in the wait for the only thing that will work, now. Hilary breaks a phrase from the tightening of the skin.

"We're ready. Just tell us what to do."

"Please," gasps Lance, "Look at us. We're ready, more than ever. Please help us...before..."

Polly reaches under the table for the box. She's satisfied that things will be moving along according to plan. Time to take a little

143

pity. They may not enjoy the tightening of her fists around their need, but the euphoria of recall will place the loosening of the senses, the relief of release, foremost in the memory if at any point they cease to play by her rules. A leveler was therefore necessary at this point; to ease the jolts and have them fit to deal with a few specifics.

Contracts must be drawn. Letters must be sent. Chambers must be furnished, beds made, keys stamped. She prefers to keep her clients as far from the legwork as possible, and there's nothing to be done but to seat them in front of the screen with a selection of refreshments. First, though, some introductions.

Polly sends Mike to fetch Angelo and Damien. They arrive as eager for work as Christian, grin wide enough to outstrip the smears of red paint across their mouths.

"Angelo, Damien: this is Lance, and Hilary, new team members. They are now looking for involvement to its full capacity – would you be so kind as to make a few phone calls? Neither will be returning to work on Monday."

Neither says a word, extracting the necessary information through turns of head and quizzical eyes. It's as easy as acquiring a few details. Names are mined from the surface memory of the pair. Hilary will no longer have to pander to Jensen: he and Cathy, the whole plastic kingdom of the advertising office, have melted into the past. Lance empties his wallet out onto the table, offering up a pile of defunct business cards to the watching mimes. House keys pass from limp hands without protest, as Lance passes over his useless and translucent personal space. Hilary feels a twinge of regret at giving up her music collection, but it passes when Polly reminds them of what they stand to gain.

"I'll send my girls along with the others to collect anything you feel you cannot do without, but remember – this is a theatre. Anything you could want or wish for by way of entertainment, magic and maquillage is here for the taking."

Their case is as simple as any she's had on board for a long time. People drop out of systems with remarkable ease without family ties to bind them – as long as paperwork remains updated, as long as bills are paid, disappearing acts are exceedingly straightforward. No faces seeking recognition, no calls from the crowd. All fans and critics shoot from the body of the group, fresh and new, carrying neither preconceptions nor memories of performers as they were before. This is what theatre is all about, unadulterated by star systems or brand loyalties.

Hilary and Lance now sit quietly, wrapped safely again in each other, wired to the screen and to the freedom from the outside world. A modest array of glasses and bottles, powders and spoons, sits with arms' reach. Polly has selected a screening from one of the calmer revues: the twins wear garlands of briar rose and soft pastel, holding two long jumping ropes between them. Christian, Angelo and Damien are in short trousers, faces painted in cherubic peaches and pinks. They perform remarkable feats over the ropes, skipping and leapfrogging across each other, ducking and diving, a trio of gyroscopes playing across the panorama, barely touching the ground.

In the dance lies a promise that is being fulfilled, deeper and quicker, within the spectators on the couch. Whilst the real-life renderings of the figures from the screen are stripping apartments and locking doors from the inside, Lance and Hilary slip further from their earthly pleasures, and bounce from ropes up into the sky.

A door swings open onto a long corridor, defying the dimensions of the building as it appears from the outside. Neither of the new inhabitants notice – it's just another province of Polly's nebulous kingdom.

Passing through the opening, tiny bells tinkle from a rope draped over the doorframe. Hilary glances upward, enchanted, and swirls her arms through the air in time with the delicate notes. Lance keeps his arms locked tight around her waist. His eyes are fixed on the carpet, patterned in peacock-coloured paisley. It laps around his ankles, threatening to swallow him up.

Most of the doors along the hallway are closed, but through the few cracks left ajar there issues a hubbub of carnival whisper. Low, throaty chuckles mingle with chinking chords from dusty organs, matches rasp over shuffling papers. Occasional splashes of colour filter through the gaps; helter-skelter of harlequin flashes, mashed up with greying skin and the gleam from polyester hairpieces. The corridor stops at a double door, presumably leading back out onto a stairwell, but the heavy chain and padlock, looped over the handles thrice over, renders useless any further speculation.

Two stops before the passage terminates, another door lies amenably open. Christian, a few steps ahead, turns to face his charges, then cocks both hands toward the vacant room, bowing slightly as he does so.

"These are your quarters," Polly proclaims from behind, "I'm sure you'll find them most adequate to your needs. There's a shower room and toilet adjoining. There's a shared Jacuzzi and steam bath back there," she gestures over her shoulder at one of the closed doors, "but I think you'd prefer to get settled in your own room first before meeting the neighbours."

Hilary and Lance nod mutely, eyes fixed on the plush king-size bed, swimming with pillows and spreads in jewelled satin. They are in desperate need of rest – the chemicals may counter exhaustion in the short term, but sleep cries for attention, borne along by the power of suggestion.

Teak panelling dominates one wall, sliding back at Polly's ministration to reveal a series of slatted shelves, upon which several items of male and female clothing lie folded, all in black, white and navy, with a few pieces in muted shades of stone, beige, ivory, eggshell and pastel blue. Hilary vaguely recognizes a jersey dress, a turtleneck, a faded denim jacket. Lance recognizes nothing; stripped of power ties and statement cufflinks, his wardrobe becomes a set of prison garb, the way it always really had been. In another compartment, two sets of cotton loungewear snuggle up, hooded tops embracing pants; both black, both form-fitting, both with elastic waistbands, no drawstrings. There are no hooks, no clothes-rail. The full-length mirror on the back of the door is made of plastic; peered into too closely; it stretches and warps the reflected figures to grotesque parodies of themselves. Lance and Hilary do not notice; having absorbed the contents of the wardrobe, their eyes and minds are further subdued, craving sleep all the more.

At the foot of the bed sits a writing desk with a single chair, another red velvet detainee from the auditorium. Upon the desk, a pot of felt-tip pens and a pile of lined paper with an empty box in each corner.

"This is for your own use," murmurs Polly, "However, anything you wish to be posted must be stamped by myself before it leaves the building. I can't allow any unsolicited information to make its way into the public eye; I'm sure you'll concur."

Again the nodding, eyelids increasingly heavy, chins hitting chests as the pair struggle to stay awake.

"Other than that, it's fairly simple. You'll pick up any other regulations along the way. You may come and go as you please, provided you check in and out with myself or another member of staff. Meals are at nine a.m., twelve thirty and six p.m. respectively. Your doses will be first thing in the morning, mid-afternoon and as often as necessary in the evening. I'll be working closely with you to work out the best combination for all involved. Now – have you any questions?"

Lance shuffles his head into an upright position, the better to fix Polly with his pleading stare, the best he can manage around his tic-frazzled eyes. He points to the bed with his free hand, whispering in awe.

"Is that...ours?"

Polly chuckles, in a gruesome parody of an indulgent maiden aunt.

"You both must be very tired. There will be plenty of time for discussion later on, if need be, but for now I shall leave you to get accustomed to your new dwelling."

She slides another teak panel, smaller than the others, fixed over the light-switch. Beneath is a pair of push buttons, one glowing dull red, the other lime green. The red has a tiny wire cage over the top, presumably to prevent false alarms.

"Push the green button if you need anything," she chirps, "and someone will be right along. Oh..." She thrusts an arm into the opposite sleeve, withdrawing a package. There is no cellophane, this time. There is no need; choice has fallen away, leaving only necessity. Opening a drawer in the writing table, she removes a set of works – a porcelain tray, pewter dish, silver straws in a shot-glass and a sheaf of slim cutting cards wrapped in linen napkins. She places the packet into the dish, and bows, backing toward the door. She does not draw any curtains; there are neither spectators, nor windows from which to look.

"Sleep well," she murmurs, "I need you on top form for your next performance."

The aides have long gone, and Polly closes the door gently, leaving Hilary and Lance to their solitude. It's everything they've always wanted, and they are barely here to sense more than a passing glow of blissful ignorance.

Hilary presses her hands to her face, teasing out another yawn. She slumps onto Lance's shoulder, the grip on her arms slackening. He is standing erect purely by default, having had no alternative, and her added weight tips the balance over and onto the bedclothes. As before, comfort wins out. They warm numb flesh with exhausted breath, rattling over stale clothing and static glimpses of naked skin. Sense memory prevails, enough to lock familiar grooves into place; chin to clavicle, arm to waist, facing but never seeing, blank stares over opposing shoulders.

Locked into a touch without touching, they no longer wait for morning. They simply wait and respire, storing energy for what will be, what has been, a rousing performance. They wait, and fend off the creeping shadows as they emerge from beneath the bed.

Days sweep past as the weekend drops into a void. Nothing remarkable happens: nothing can, it's all been done before. Hilary and Lance become names on envelopes, the occasional decorative scrawl across a cheque. They don't miss much, nothing much misses them. They plunge into binary on the outside, and awaken on the inside to gaping vesicles and consequence-free sensory experience.

Part XVIII

The more Evan hears about Carrie's ties to the theatre, the higher his amazement cranks at her disinterest in performing. He has seen her spin, and felt the power she traps between each fine hair across her skin. He doesn't quite want to hinge his argument on his own keen observations; he's not ready yet to be caught looking. He opts instead for lines of reasoning founded in her clout; of having the building under her control.

"Are you kidding me? You could make a killing – name in lights and all that jazz."

Illuminated only by the glow of her cigarette, Carrie screws her face up in distaste.

"Man, I have a hard enough time knowing who I am in real life – I couldn't handle a whole bunch of other personalities at the same time."

They sit out back, in the alley behind the theatre. Carrie knows her privileges within the building could probably stretch to smoking inside, but only in Polly's quarters. She'd much rather come outside than spend more time than she needs to with the grand high directress.

"I kind of know what you mean. I used to think that actors took their roles off the same way you'd take off your clothes – but everyone I've met in here seems to be in character, all the time. Polly, too, and she's not even an actress. I've only met her a couple of times, but…it's like she's onstage, running through lines written by somebody else. "

Carrie nods – sometimes it takes an outsider to point out the obvious.

"When you think about it, she's been doing this for a long time. I mean, she's my grandmother's age, older. When you're stuck in a character for that length of time, it can't be easy to just…go back to normal. It'd be like a total anticlimax."

They both ponder this for a moment or two: the efforts and risks involved in creating a personality arresting enough to inhabit indefinitely.

"It would be a bit of a come-down. How could you just...go about your life, like normal, knowing that you've had these roles to move about in?"

"That's the thing," replies Carrie, "They don't. None of the old-timers ever leave the theatre for long – they sleep here, eat here, drink here. Polly hasn't set foot outside the door since Christ knows when. I mean, for example, how'd you hear about the job?"

Evan's eyes furl in skepticism.

"It was up on the Internet. But so's everything, these days. That doesn't mean they're all stuck in here, like some freaky reenactment of the Donner Party."

Carrie takes a long draw, making room for movement within the argument.

"I didn't say that. What I am saying is that there's a big old world out there, and they take zero interest in any of it. Here before I get here, here before I leave. No traveling revues. No flyers for any other attractions in the city. This place is sealed off to anything or anyone that might fuck with Polly's...*ambience.*"

Evan sees it, but doesn't want to believe it. He turns the conversation elsewhere, keen to avoid pissing Carrie off.

"I admit it's a bit...cloistered, compared to other places I've seen. It doesn't matter anyway, neither of us wants to act, and I don't plan to tend bar for the rest of my life. What about you, though? If you're not an aspiring thespian, what do you want to be?"

Carrie laughs, nearly choking on her cigarette. She grabs the edge of the keg tightly, to steady herself and formulate a reply.

"God, why is it that everyone has to want to *be* something? I don't have a fucking clue what I want to be, all I know is what I like. You say you don't want to tend bar for the rest of your life? What, then? You got some grand plan instead?"

He feels the sting of having spoken out of line. This almost clouds his joy at hearing that she's equally clueless, foundering in a mass of possibilities and prescriptions.

"I'm sorry, Carrie. Didn't mean to put you on the spot. I don't have a clue, either. I took up my degree thinking I wanted to be a journalist – now I'm not so sure."

Every career path and buzzword espoused by the guidance counselors and recruitment agencies hangs in the air before them, broken stars spilling their glitter to earth. Nowadays, kids no longer dreamt of space travel, of digging for treasure in Aztec kingdoms, of strolling from blazes bearing rescue victims. They didn't even dance around their bedrooms the way they once did, singing into microphones. Choices were still limitless, but with more and more vocations piling in to meet the demand of the new age, these arduous pursuits seemed to take more than they gave. There was something more attractive in taking top tables in boardrooms, and mugging into web-cams promised to fast-track stardom. All or nothing, and nobody settled anymore for anything less than recognition, and the accoutrements to match. Ambition became a game of wanting to *have*. Toothsome coveting and scrambling makes it that much more difficult to admit that, for the most part, nobody really knew what they wanted to *be*. Carrie and Evan swim gratefully in this brief connection of mutual uncertainty.

A light appears on the second floor of the building, casting a sickly orange pall over the seated pair. Evan checks his watch, no longer under any illusion as to where the regulars disappear to after last orders. It's coming up for two a.m.

"What do you think they're doing up there?"

"Christ knows. When my grandmother ran the place, back when it was still a teeny bit legal, she used to have everyone up to her room for a smoke."

Evan can tell by the crooked grin that Carrie isn't talking tobacco.

"Yeah? Can't imagine folks back then all giggly and mashed on weed."

"Not weed, my friend. They were a lot more refined back then – used to smoke opium. Can you imagine it? After the show, everyone who was anyone in the theatre in Scotland sitting with my gran, chilling out and getting loaded...amazing. Wish I'd been there."
"You think that's what they're up to upstairs?"

Carrie laughs. Polly and opium is not a combination that springs easily to mind without attendant hilarity.

"Nah – it's not her thing. I don't know what she's up to. Probably just plying them all with brandy and asking for money. Either that or some freaky swingers club – if that's the case, I'd rather not know."

This bliss of elected ignorance is rare enough to be savored. Nothing is secret anymore, what with prices attached to the slightest sliver of scandal. Sometimes it's a relief to pretend that everything sits pertly in it's proper place, functioning just fine without peering eyes and furtive gossip. They breathe the cold of the settling city, purer now that the traffic has slowed, the magic of the witching hours allowing space to swallow silent air.

Evan tries again.

"So what do you like?"

"I don't think anyone can answer that neatly. I like everything, I like nothing – I suppose if I was filling in a form…"

She drifts off, more unsure than ever.

"I get it. It's nice to have room to move around, change your mind."

"Art. Books. Music. Theatre, sometimes. But that doesn't make what I like any different to the preferences of a billion other people."

"But you are."

The combinations lie in the small print. A love or like mixed up with the innocuous – in Carrie's case, a cold gin on a hot day, green jelly babies, the smell of pencil sharpenings. The hatred of intolerance, gossip, cheap magazines, yellow wine gums, prom dresses, powerlessness, the vague sensation that sometimes she's spinning on an axis wildly out of synch with the rest of the planet.

"Yeah…we're all different. Everyone's unique. Talk about your contradictions in terms. Your turn, mate. What do you like?"

Evan remains as tentative as ever on every front but one.

"Well…I'm still not sure of what I want to be, or what I want.

But I do know one thing that I like."

Like is enough. Enough is a gift. Doors open gently onto dark alleys and catwalks, mausoleums and bedrooms, enough to keep moving, out and away. Enough for bad dreams, enough for paranoia, and sufficient distance to run, away from the masks and cellophane. They may be unashamedly high, defiantly hooked, but here in the dark they breathe and laugh and sigh and stir all on their own, neither need nor want to seal the place off, bricked up in holes in collapsing walls.

He reaches over carefully, conscious of the glowing cone of cigarette ash clutched between her fingers. He places a hand over hers. She doesn't flinch. By the light from the auditorium upstairs, her eyes hold a promise that imagination doesn't have to be the death of them.

Part XIX

Carrie paints faster and wider and brighter than ever before, making up for lost time, opening new portals. The cartoon portraits have been scrapped. She's tired of etching wails into the wind, when the screams are not her own anymore. She paints now what she likes, and there's more to choose from than she'd imagined.

It's getting dark outside. Her reflection in the window, under the fluorescent strip-light, is headier and in more dimensions than the pane can hold, as she ducks and dives, pokes and jabs. She squeezes colour and shape, paint and curiosity, viscosity and desire from the tubes, smearing with brushes, with fingers, stray elbows and escaped strands of hair, jolting and streaming like espresso.

A figure watches from the doorway, unseen, unheard. Carrie has an MP3 player in her back pocket, and is lost to the world, ears and eyes and hands fully occupied with the task at hand. Mrs Halliday shakes her head in disbelief, an unchecked smile fleeting across her usual sobriety. She has come to give Carrie yet another warning about her attendance, but this spectacle confirms her hunch – the renegade detention princess is beyond the trappings of the school, the rules therein. Desperate to watch the picture emerge, she forces a withdrawal, as silent as her entry. This was too special, too curious, too precious to risk derailing with a sharp cough, a wooden ruler thumping a desk. She continues to shake her head as she eases the door closed, wondering, not for the first time, if the job will cease to plant landmines of astonishment in the turgid topsoil of the identikit days.

Carrie can't see anything but colour, splashes, explosions of liquid energy. The music in her ears appears as strokes and blobs of dripping paint, edging up and across the canvas, running down her forearms, enveloping her in successions of sensory phenomena.

The change came on that morning. She was not in the habit of reliving conversations, tweaking out areas of importance, but Evan's questions continued to ring in her ears long after their lips parted, echoed in her head the whole way home, long after she fell, giddily, into bed, and woke her up that morning with a smile.

This is it – she paints what she likes, simple, childish, artistry stripped back to primary colours. And it's the best she's ever done. She can't figure out why, is yet to get used to the sensation of having another in mind. Before, painting by herself, she was excellent, technically faultless. Now, painting with him seated on her shoulder, in her head, in her heart, she is phenomenal. Everything on the canvas lives and moves, it thrums with the electricity of more than one soul. In giving a little of herself over, she has gained in something ineffable, unaccountable, and utterly breathtaking.

Sunday dawns, the sunshine passing undetected over Carrie's sleeping form until half past noon. She wakes to a sudden pressure at the foot of the bed, a gentle hand on a shoulder. She jerks upright, barely missing a crack of cranium to septum with the looming presence.

"Jesus! You gave me fright." Tracy pulls back, cackling, and places a package on Carrie's lap.

"Happy birthday, hen."

Tracy hasn't done this for about ten years. The midnight courier act got old pretty quickly when Carrie deduced that Father Christmas was a fabrication. It was elementary, really – a combination of rumours at school with the aromatic evidence of Santa's brandy on the breath of her parents. After her father left, birthday and Christmas gifts materialised days late, roughly wrapped if at all, accompanied by a sheepish grin and a promise of some cash in hand later.

"Oh…cheers, mum."

This is awkward; the closeness feels vaguely interrogatory, invasive. Carrie wonders whether she's in trouble for something, then chalks up the sensation to novelty.

"Aren't you going to open it?"

"Oh – right, yeah. Thanks, by the way, you didn't have to."

"Don't be daft. It's a big day, a special birthday."

Her eighteenth. She's beset by a new string of conventions, harangued by a new set of laws and responsibilities. It's supposed to be a moment of becoming something real – she's now expected to be an adult, and she's never felt less ready.

The package is fairly lightweight, and defiantly box-shaped in the face of a myriad of geometrical nightmares; all the cones, cylinders, tetrahedrons, dreamed up by manufacturing execs in the throes of boredom.

Tracy has wrapped it beautifully, too – she's evidently been working toward this little presentation over a fairly commendable period of sobriety. No pink, either – the paper is a silky royal blue, neatly folded, no glimpse of sticky tape evident. A matching blue ribbon – wide satin, no holographic plastic – binds the corners, creating an objet d'art of the kind Carrie's almost afraid to touch.

"It's gorgeous, mum – I don't want to open it!"

Tracy bows her head with a shy smile. She's still riding on a sense of obligation to make up for lost time, and is pleased to have achieved a small success. It's always been difficult to surprise her daughter; after a while, she stopped trying. Now there blossoms a hope that perhaps she can do right by her; by no means fixing broken years, but sketching in a little space for manoeuvre. Making good for once paves a path of allowance for incoming fuck-ups, salves the conscience for a spell, makes a marker of a dry patch in preparation for further wet ones.

"Come on, come on – here, we'll both do it."

Then, like an image on a neutered greetings card, Carrie and her mother each pluck an end of the ribbon and pull, unlocking the gift. Carrie flicks a fingernail under the edge of the paper, folding and tearing with the delicacy of a practiced joint-roller.

The brown cardboard box inside requires nothing more than unfolding. The contents are padded and tangled with shredded tissue paper, necessitating a root around for something solid. She withdraws a roll of canvas, tied together with burlap twine, which falls apart to reveal a set of professional quality paintbrushes.

"Wow, mum, these are amazing!"

For the first time since she was a child, Carrie's enthusiasm needs no simulation. She is at a loss for words, rarely in receipt of something that hits the mark so perfectly. Decent art supplies were expensive, well out of Carrie's league. Even if she'd had the cash, she'd probably refrain from such purchases; courtesy of a luxury-checking mechanism inbuilt from growing up under a roof where scraping by was the general order of things.

"There's more in there," Tracy mumbles, "Just a couple of wee things."

Carrie tips the box out onto the bed. A cluster of hair grips, a bottle of ebony nail polish, and a small velvet jewellery box.

This latter opens to reveal a silver locket on a long filigree chain, peppered with light flecks of tarnish between chips of rhinestone. It's fucking horrible, either a gaudy relic or some retro-fied imitation of one, but Carrie grins through her distaste. Tracy has never given her jewellery, ever, and this is evidently a statement of sorts.

"Woah. Mum, this must have cost a fortune…"

Tracy sighs, a delicate theatrical murmur of compromise.

"It belonged to your gran. I've kept it for years. Wanted to throw it down the shitter after your dad left, but I hung on to it, just in case..." she doesn't elaborate on any imagined contingency. "Well, if it belongs to anyone, it's you, Carrie. I know you're set to inherit something a lot…grander, but I though this'd be a nice wee token to start with. You don't have to wear it or anything; I just know your dad would have wanted you to have it."

Carrie removes the locket from the box, unsure whether or not to slip it on. Going by the look on Tracy's face, this is difficult enough without the constant presence of a totem around Carrie's neck. She runs her thumbnail between the hinges, splitting it open. There's a faded photograph of Zinnia is one half. She looks about Carrie's age, make-up pasted on lips and eyes evident even in sepia. The other half of the locket is empty, awaiting the image of the next bearer.

"Thanks, mum," Carrie whispers, folding the locket back into the box, placing it aside. She'd figure out what to do with it later.

"So!" Tracy bursts into some athletically false cheer, "What you getting up to for your big day? Any plans?"

"Well…I was going to see if I could get a few words with Polly. I mean, I'm not desperate, and I'm not sure what to do with all the legal shite, but it'd help to know where I stand."

Tracy shakes her head, searching her internal catalogue of parental aphorisms and anecdotes from problem pages for some advice.

"Em…all I can say is, get everything in writing. Read about a fella who lost his job, his house, his car, all because he signed something in the wrong place."

"Oh, I'm not up for anything like that today. All I want is a chat, maybe book a time to talk it over. Best case scenario would be if she hangs around, helps me out. I don't have a bloody clue how to run a business – all I'm good for in there is knocking up cocktails and calming down the nutters at last orders."

"Whatever you do, be careful. I don't trust that woman, she's a few fritters short of a butty, if you get what I mean. Besides, that's not what I meant. It's your birthday – don't you have a party or a pub crawl planned? You not going up the dancing for your first legal bevvie?"

Carrie suppresses a shriek of laughter. Leaving aside the redundancy of the legal beverage, she refrains from informing Tracy that the very thought of entering a Glasgow nightclub makes her skin crawl. She does have plans, though.

"A…mate of mine works at the theatre. I'm gonna hang about for a bit and see what the crack is. Maybe hit the pub if he finishes early enough."

"Sounds…nice," Tracy replies, more sure than ever that her daughter ambles along through a universe irreparably parallel to her own. "Well, have fun."

She leans forward, wrapping her daughter in a dutifully reciprocated hug. Carrie's agenda may not be electric, but it does leave a decent twelve-hour window of solitude, an empty house in which Tracy can cook in her own juices without reproach.

Mother-daughter bonding session drawing to a close, Tracy leaves the room and defects to her own. She shakes a blue capsule from a bottle and leans back on her bed, exhausted by this soul-baring recital, grateful that it occurs just once a year. She jerks the blinds closed with one hand, and sinks into sleep, safe in the knowledge that there are now two adults capable of pulling the strings up to adequate functionality.

Carrie ponders grabbing a few more hours of rest. Instead, she shoots out of bed and into the shower, pummelling life into her eighteen years with each handful of shampoo, each jet of hot water. It would be kind of cool to buy smokes without ID, kind of reassuring to know she can stroll into any licensed premises she chooses, kind of grown-up to be able to vote, but other than that – pretty unremarkable. Soon the doormat will be adrift in council tax bills, offers from credit-card companies, and those pink tear-off envelopes inviting her to get a swab jammed up her vagina. The rest is trash – porn movies, strip clubs, proper shoes, job interviews, life-shattering decisions to be made as to what the hell she wants to do with herself. Dull, fetid, useless accoutrements. So what.

She lifts her face to the stream, losing track of time. When she finally steps out into the murky bathroom, shaking off like drenched cat, she feels the weight of the theatre pressing down. She doesn't want it. She doesn't need it. She desires nothing more from the place than for Polly to maintain the status quo, the freedom to come and go as she pleases and a guaranteed perch at the bar to watch Evan work.

She dresses with care, each motion uncharacteristically jerky and awkward from lack of practice. Underwear is easy enough, but the rest requires some thought. Rubbing a towel over her hair, teasing the soaking silk into damp felt, she selects her least-worn pair of jeans and a simple white shirt, laying them out on the bed along with a pair of nearly-new black patent kitten heels. She stares at the flattened portrait as though contemplating a corpse, a stranger's clothes, a grown-ups attire. She thrusts the towel aside and slips into the gear, feeling stiff and stuffed and itching with formality.

She takes a bag and folds into it a change for later – Pixies T-shirt, combat trousers, ripped Converse hi-tops. Better.

She draws the line at make-up. Opening a box of cosmetics, into which she discharges any items given as ill-advised gifts, she searches for a colour that doesn't scream of desperation or harlotry. Everything is bright red, candy pink, peacock blue, tangerine bronze, swirled together in comic-book kitsch. She closes the box and compromises by drying her hair with an electric dryer, smoothing the hair cuticles as neatly as she can with a near-toothless comb.

She stands back to inspect the apparition, freaking herself out. Evan won't recognise her. She looks like an adult: a proper fucking church-going, upstanding member of society. She practices moving her face into expressions to match, with which to address Polly later on. It's like watching a ventriloquist's dummy moving around with her face grafted on. She shudders, shakes her head in disgust and grabs a jacket. May as well get this going – the sooner she's had her little conference with the directress, the sooner she can slip back into worn cotton and applied irony.

She picks up her mobile phone and rings Evan.

"Hello?"

"Hey, it's me."

"Carrie! Happy birthday!"

"Cheers. Listen, I know you're working tonight, but I'm going down now-ish to have a few words with our favourite basket-case. Care to join? May be go for a drink or a smoke afterward?"

Evan can barely contain his glee, casting up a prayer of thanks for the blind interface of the telephone. It may not be dinner and a show, but it's a deliberate placement of the two in a context beyond the incidental.

"Sure, sounds great. I have a gift for you, too. Meet you in an hour?"

"See you then."

Carrie doesn't stare from the windows of the bus, despite the sun bestowing its forgiving golden sheen to the sandstone buildings. She's too caught up in thought, wishing for an easy out, a reprieve, an extra few years in which to substantiate the statistics of adulthood with something more solid than a date of birth.

She walks from the bus stop to the theatre on borrowed feet, as uncomfortable in her newly acquired year as in her squeaky shoes. Evan waits on the bottom step, looking equally strange in a flannel shirt, jeans and trainers – she's never seen him in anything but his uniform. He stands as she approaches, a gift bag slung over one wrist.

"Hey!" he begins, wrapping her in a warm hug, kissing a fold of hair in the crook of her neck. "Happy birthday. Wow…you look great! Different."

This is not what she wants to hear. She's grateful for a change of subject.

"Thanks! What's going on in there – how come the door's locked up?"

Evan shakes his head at the drawn blinds and padlocks.

"I've no idea. It's still early, though – maybe they're cleaning or rehearsing or something. Don't they close to the public during the day?"

Carrie shrugs, racking it up to another of Polly's caprices. He hands her the bag, bowing his head under his mass of hair as he does so, still conscious of her latent fire.

She flashes a coy incisor, nibbling her lip. She's still not used to this new way of things, the giving and receiving of signals and long looks over dusky eyelashes.

"Thank you."

She splits the tape across the top, and withdraws a small wooden object, arrowed slats and screws, with a short ledge bridging either side. Looking at him curiously, she shakes the bag, still weighty enough to contain more. Three small canvas panels, each three inches square, the breadth of the bridge. A tiny paintbrush, toothpick slender, bristles finer than spider webs. It's a studio in miniature – an pocket-sized easel with the works. A sound explodes from her chest, one with which she is unfamiliar – she laughs in tinkling delight.

"Oh my god, that's so..." she holds back overused trash-talk, returning 'adorable', 'cute' and 'dope' to the magazine shit-pile from whence they came, "...fucking *cool*."

Evan relaxes, visibly, shoulders dropping from around his ears.

"Thank you," she says again, making room for each word to make its mark, forming a real message instead of churning out an automatic response. "I've never seen anything like this before. It's beautiful."

"I saw it in the university art store, and thought you could use it – you know, on the go. It's pretty, but...it's nothing yet. Not until you've painted it."

Then comes the Hollywood kiss. It should really be raining as they stand beneath a golf umbrella, or against a backdrop of hallucinogenic sunset. But it's four in the afternoon, it's a Glasgow side street, and their kiss is sound-tracked by the thumping bass and whooping expletives of a passing Renault full of drunken football fans, perfumed with the odour of stale cooking fat from the kebab shop two doors down. It's still a magic of its own kind, though, as they each press tightly against the other, an alliance against the passing meltdown of the urban decay. Carrie has never had a birthday worth celebrating, and here, now, arrives a cause.

When they pull apart, the ghost of the building still looms, closed off, averting its shuttered eyes. It's an inconvenient truth, but Evan does have to show up to work at some point this evening. Still, there's time.

"So...did you still want to get that drink?"

"Sure." Carrie holds the bag aloft. "Just let me get the fuck out of this...penguin suit."

Part XX

Through a slit in the purple drapes over the second floor porthole, a green eye glimmers over the parting couple. Polly has always known this day was coming, and has long ago made necessary preparations.

Carrie will get over it. She can tell by the jaunt in the hands clasped tightly that she will be plenty occupied, at least for the immediate future. Plus, the insurance money would keep her sweet, once the investigations had exempted her from any involvement in the conflagration.

So far, it has taken three trips in the minivan, time added on to allow for each change of registration plate. Two more should do it, she should think. The performers had been as docile as expected, shuffling along the corridor in stocking feet, gazing up at the ceiling. A trip outside of any sort was a novelty and privilege, not to be sniffed at.

It was a great pity about the Pantheon, of course – she has grown attached to the place over the years, and the animals especially will find the change somewhat distressing. But there is no other way, not now.

There will always be derelict buildings, gaps in narrative, rabbit holes and wardrobe doors in which such worlds as hers may exist, sight unseen. There will always be cracks in the pavement through which to slip – they were artists, after all, as comfortably at one with the weeds as the orchids, if the script so dictates.

Props, scenery, costumes and seats are to be left behind. Their absence would be too conspicuous to anyone sifting through the remains. They mean nothing anyway – Polly and her family have all they need – they *are* all they need. They are adequately sedated for the time being, but the real kick comes from inside. The rest is merely a prompt. Zinnia and Polly knew it long ago, back when the marble out front still shone in the wet, before the moths began to chew the drapes. The essence of the self needs a platform from which to speak. There it stands, on the stage, amid the blood and tears, the distillation of unadulterated character. Running into nothingness, Polly's patients perform the remarkable feat of standing under spotlight, cemented with every ministration into what they really are. The power of the performance transcends the drug, providing a high equal to no other, a daily full-body cleanse and exorcism found in no other forum, in no other sphere. It's a pretty fair bargain, she thinks, and this relocation is but a minor inconvenience.

Sharp notes of petrol catch the back of her throat, kicking up lashes of steam in her windpipe. Not much longer. Two more trips, maybe three.

She turns from the window, pulling the drapes down with her into the puddle at her feet, as she stalks down the corridor and into the performers' wing. On the other side of the double doors, she laces the heavy chain back through the door handles. There's really no need, not anymore, but it doesn't do to let standards slip, even this close to the end. On her way to her chamber, almost fully stripped, now, she peeks around the doors of the few remaining occupied rooms. She saves her favourites until last.

Lance and Hilary sit calmly on the edge of the bed, wearing their lounging suits as ordered. Each will move and breathe in nothing but the aura of the other. Polly could strike a match right there in the room, and they would not stir.

His hands are locked on her waist. Her arms clutch his shoulders like a life-preserver. Unmoving, they barely flicker for breath, posed in still-life as though captured in a camera fade. It's the eyes, though, dripping from the frame, in open supplication. Awaiting a cue, awaiting a surge, they still fall into one another, falling and falling over again.

Polly smiles, and closes the door once more on the static dream. Then onto her chamber, for one final look around. No whispers remain of any *nepenthe*; true to its nature, it has seeped into the realm of the forgotten.

THE END

Author Biography

Kirsty Neary was born in 1986, and grew up in and around Glasgow. After a few false starts seeking to assuage the boredom of suburbia, she settled on writing as her preferred medium in which to invest her creativity. She attends the University of Glasgow, studying English Literature, Film and Television studies. She currently lives in Hamilton.

Printed in the United Kingdom by
Lightning Source UK Ltd., Milton Keynes
142165UK00001B/59/P